D0018131

# RIVEROFINK
# ZENITH

# RIVEROFINK
# ZENITH

# HELEN DENNIS

Illustrated by
BONNIE KATE WOLF

*Hodder
Children's
Books*

Hodder Children's Books
An imprint of Hachette Children's Group
Part of Hodder & Stoughton
Carmelite House
50 Victoria Embankment
London EC4Y 0DZ

An Hachette UK Company
www.hachette.co.uk

For Steve . . . Always.
Thank you for your
light, laughter and love!

'Architecture has recorded the great ideas of the human race.

Not only every religious symbol but every human thought has its page in that vast book.'

— Victor Hugo

# DAY 57
## 25th April

Jed was going to live for ever.

There *was* a glitch in the plan. An obstacle to overcome. But if that was solved, then he'd never die. He'd already survived imprisonment in a cage, drowning (twice), and drinking poison. So it was ironic that he was now travelling in the back of a death wagon.

Death was part of the plan. Dying in the River Neckar meant Jed and Kassia would escape NOAH, the organisation that wanted to know Jed's secret. His secret at that exact moment was that neither of them was dead at all. Truth was, they were both very much alive.

'You go Teufelsstein, right?' The driver called over his shoulder to where Jed and Kassia were sitting hunched together on a hospital trolley. Jed was trying

1

hard not to think about all the dead people who'd been carried in the back of the van before him. He looked down at the scrap of paper Charlie Monalees had given them before they'd left the hospital. 'That's what it says here. That's a town, right?' Jed had no idea where they were but they'd been on the road for at least half an hour. Charlie had obviously asked his driver friend to get them as far away from the hospital as possible.

'Not town. What you say in English? Beauty spot,' explained the driver in his heavy German accent. Then he laughed a little as if use of the word 'beauty' was particularly funny and part of a joke they should have understood.

Kassia looked across at Jed as if seeking reassurance.

'We go miles from Heidelberg,' went on the driver. 'It's fun yes.'

*Fun* was not the word Jed would have chosen. But the driver was obviously finding the novelty of being able to chat to his passengers highly entertaining. The screened section between the back of the van and the three seats at the front had been slid wide open. Jed watched as the driver glanced up at the rear-view mirror then knitted his eyebrows together as if he was troubled by what he saw.

'Everything OK?' Jed asked.

The driver looked back over his shoulder. 'Not sure. Motorbike very close. I not like.'

'You think we're being followed?'

The driver wrinkled his face and then shrugged. 'We find out,' he said. He leant heavily on the accelerator and shoved the gearstick forward. 'Hold on tight now!'

Jed gripped his fingers round the edge of the trolley.

The van thundered ahead and then lunged to the left. Jed and Kassia rocked to the side and Jed's arm smacked against the wall of the van.

'Is the bike still there?' demanded Kassia. 'We can't see.'

The driver threw the van a little faster to the left before he answered. 'He's still there.'

Jed's arm thumped again on the inside wall of the van. The back of a death wagon was not the best place to be if you were involved in a high-speed chase. Passenger safety for dead people was clearly not high on the list of priorities but as Jed's arm thudded against the metal interior for the third time, he wished the back of the van had been fitted with seat-belts. And he wished he could see the road. There was a very real chance he was going to be sick. He looked at Kassia. Her face was turning green.

The van shifted once more to the left and the gears

groaned as the driver forced the vehicle faster.

'We should get in the front,' said Jed, pointing one hand towards the open screened section, whilst gripping tight to the underside of the trolley with the other hand.

'*Really?*' Clambering through a tight space while the van was racing down the motorway was clearly not at the top of Kassia's wish list.

The van lurched again and a black body bag ripped up from the storage space under the trolley, unfolded, and flapped towards them.

Kassia cowered backwards as the bag sheathed itself around her shoulders.

'Seriously! We need to get into the front!' Jed strained upwards from the trolley and flung himself to the opening in the partition. He held his hand to Kassia and she pulled at the body bag that had tangled itself round her like a cloak. It flapped free for a moment and then pinned itself against Jed's torso as Kassia manoeuvred herself through the opening and launched into the front seat.

'Good move,' said the driver as he floored the accelerator again.

Jed was thrown forward so that his face crunched hard against the section of plastic screening that had not been slid back. 'Nice,' he muttered, his cheek pinned against the screen so that only half his face could move.

'Take my hand,' yelled Kassia.

Jed wrestled back from the screen and grabbed for Kassia's arm. The body bag was now beating around his shoulders like wings. He tugged hard on Kassia's hand and hauled himself through the opening, the body bag thrashing and flailing behind him. The hole in the panel was small, Jed was bigger than Kassia and the space in the front he was trying to climb into was more crowded now she was there. He could hardly breathe. He rolled sideways on to his back and thrust his shoulders downwards, turning his head to the right. Out of the side window he could see they were flashing past traffic. They were pulling alongside a bus to the right of them. A small girl was staring hard out of the window. Jed tried to smile as he pushed himself further through the hole, his body crumpling so that he was now face forward, pressed against the window. The body bag ballooned up behind him. His eyes locked on the girl's in the bus.

The girl recoiled. She bunched her fists in front of her mouth; her eyes widened. Jed tried to work out why she was looking so horrified. And then the realisation hit him. She thought he was climbing out of the body bag! That she was watching someone come back from the dead!

Jed grappled with the body bag and tried to smile reassuringly at her, but the speed of the van and the pressure of his face against the window pane was contorting his lips. His tongue lolled to the side. The little girl was clearly not reassured!

'You OK?' yelped Kassia, finally ripping the body bag free and tossing it into the footwell before helping Jed swivel round into the third front seat.

'I'm doing better than she is,' he said, pointing at the girl in the bus who was now obviously in the middle of a full-blown panic attack.

Jed tried to make his face look comforting. He failed. The girl was screaming uncontrollably now.

Jed shrugged awkwardly, reached up for the seat-belt, and clicked himself into place.

The driver seemed to take this move as encouragement. 'Now we go really fast,' he grinned.

Kassia fumbled with the latch of her own seat-belt then hung on tight to the strap.

In the rear-view mirror, Jed could see a motorbike close behind them. The driver was clad all in black, his shoulders hunched, hands gripped tight to the handle bars. But there was another bike close behind, gaining ground, weaving through the traffic, pulling alongside the other rider. The first biker acknowledged this arrival with a nod of the head.

'There are two!' Jed yelped.

'I know. I not like worry you!' said the driver, pulling away from beside the school bus and ploughing down the centre lane.

He threw the van into the inside lane and the motorbikes swerved to keep close on his tail. Then he floored the accelerator again and pulled the van back across the three lanes of motorway traffic so that the school bus and the hysterical girl were just a memory. Jed could see Kassia's fingers turning white as she gripped tight to the seat-belt. 'Isn't there a speed limit?' she yelped hopefully.

The driver grinned almost manically. 'Not in Germany!'

He wove the van between two small cars and the drivers blasted their horns. A third car braked sharply, weaving as it lurched to the right and tried to clear the lane. But the motorbikes pressed closer behind them. The gap between them was shortening.

'We try something new!' said the driver.

He pulled the van fast alongside a huge lorry that was travelling more slowly in the inside lane. Then he swung the van sharply in front of the lorry and leant heavily on the brakes. The wheels squealed and Kassia and Jed lurched forwards in their seats, the belt cutting hard across Jed's shoulder. The van slowed. All Jed could see in the rear-view mirror was the looming shape of the lorry. The lorry driver was far from happy. He thumped his horn but the driver of the death wagon did not speed up. In the shadow of the huge lorry, the van was hidden. The motorbikes raced past, their riders scanning the road, obviously confused about where the van had disappeared to.

'Nice one!' said Jed, as the lorry driver blasted his horn again.

But the cover was short-lived. One of the motorbike riders was searching over his shoulder. He'd seen the van hiding in the shadow of the lorry and was dropping his speed.

'U-oh,' said the driver. 'We try plan C.'

Jed was already sure he would not like plan C.

The driver glanced to his side, accelerated forward and ploughed down the narrow hard-shoulder lane. He undercut the slow moving traffic that was travelling down the inside lane. But the hard shoulder was narrower: the edging was uneven and the van bumped and bounced as it raced forward.

And just to the edge of his field of vision, Jed was aware of something advancing. It wasn't on the road. It was on a track that was carving sideways towards them.

A train.

Any minute now the hard shoulder would run out as the train track turned and moved parallel with the road. Jed gripped tighter to the seat-belt. The track was running right beside them, the roar of the train audible now as the carriage charged along so close that the outside edge of the van was skimming the paintwork from the train. Sparks of metal and paintwork clouded the air.

Jed could see the hard shoulder was narrowing away to nothing. 'We're going to run out of room,' he cried. If they didn't move back into the proper lane of traffic they were going to be totally sandwiched between the train and the traffic moving slowly beside them. They'd be crushed like an empty drinks can.

In front of them, traffic was bunching together. There was a four-way junction ahead. And they were running out of road. Running out of space. And running out of time.

'Hang on!' bellowed the driver.

Jed couldn't believe anyone could think such instructions were necessary! The hard shoulder was running out, the train almost close enough to buckle the side of the van completely. The junction clogged with cars. They were heading towards a major collision!

Jed pulled Kassia in beside him in an attempt to

cover her head from the impact he knew would be coming. But the driver flung the gearstick hard and yanked down on the steering wheel, turning the van at almost ninety degrees. The wheels spun and the van ricocheted forward, cutting across the front of the mass of waiting traffic, like thread passing through the eye of a needle. The van hurtled sideways across the four-way junction.

'Wahoo!' yelled the driver.

Jed had no words. Cars behind them were spinning and shifting in the van's wake. A post van slammed hard into the back of a delivery lorry, its bonnet snapping open and smoke belching out into the air. The train thundered past on the track to the side of them. And in the midst of the chaos behind, two motorbikes wove their way through the traffic.

'Ah,' winced the driver. 'Not wahoo. We still have them.'

Jed tried to breathe deeply. But he was finding it hard to do anything other than hang on.

The junction behind them, they were now off the motorway and on a narrower road leading into a town. And Jed had an even worse feeling about this than he'd had about plan C.

The road-sign welcomed them to Bad Dürkheim. Jed could think of plenty of places where he was sure he'd feel more welcome. He peered out of the window and in the wing-mirror of the van he could see both motorbikes drawing ever closer. One bike was edging to the side, slipping round on the inside. In front of them was a roundabout. The bike was obviously intending to cut off their exit.

'To the right, look!' Jed blurted.

The driver turned his head and acknowledged the presence of the bike. They were metres from the roundabout. The bike was slowing. The exit would be closed off.

But the driver of the death wagon had other ideas. 'You do it this way in England. No?' He hit the entrance to the roundabout and instead of turning with the traffic flow to the right, he depressed the throttle hard and spun the van to the left into a stream of oncoming traffic. The sound of horns was deafening. A car swerved and mounted the roundabout, churning deep furrows in the grass. A second braked so hard it was tossed into a tailspin. Both motorbikes had turned in the opposite direction and, for a second, the van was free on a narrower road and heading deeper into town.

But Kassia had seen the obstruction ahead. 'No!' she yelled. 'Watch out!'

Temporary lights were controlling the flow of traffic

around a stretch of roadworks. The light was red. But the driver of the death wagon had no intention of stopping now. He tugged down hard on the steering wheel and the van mounted the pavement, demolishing daffodils and crocuses that had been planted to line the route. But flowers weren't the only foliage in his path.

'The tree!' yelled Jed.

The trunk of a huge oak barred their route straight ahead. To the right was a deep pit in the road edged with traffic cones. A workman held a pneumatic drill in the air like an umbrella, cowering from all the rubble and earth that the van and following motor-bikes were sending tumbling into the trench he was digging. The tree was getting closer. There was only one way to avoid it.

The driver turned the wheel again and the van bounced down the curb and on to the forecourt of a petrol station set back from the road. An elderly woman was stepping tentatively out of a gleaming red BMW. Jed braced himself. The van driver screamed through the window. 'Entschuldigung!'

The old woman flung herself against the side of the car, just in time for the death wagon to career into the door she'd left open. The door was torn free of its fixings and hurtled into the air, spinning like a badly thrown frisbee.

The impact made the van shudder and for a moment the steering wheel rocked out of control. There was no time to shout another apology. The van sped along the front of the petrol-station shop, obliterating a display of newspapers. The papers cycloned up into the air and splattered on to the windscreen. 'I can't see!' yelled the driver as the newsprint obscured his view.

Kassia reached across and jabbed at the windscreen-wiper control as the driver clung tight to the wheel trying to regain control. But the speed of the van kept the newspapers splayed flat against the glass, completely erasing the sight of the road ahead.

The driver yelled again, probably something very impolite in German. The only view out of the window was of repeated photographs of the German chancellor and headlines printed again and again in large red print.

Jed marvelled at the fact that no visibility at all didn't mean the driver felt the need to slow the van down. Whether the papers were moved or not, he intended to keep driving.

Jed frantically unclipped his seat-belt, wound down his window and stretched out of the van, snatching at the newspapers and dragging them away from the screen. The wipers swiped backwards and forwards at his hand. 'Turn them off!' he yelled at Kassia.

She grimaced and the wipers stopped just as the van swung sharply round a bend in the road. Jed lurched back from the windscreen just enough to see that the motorbikes were still behind them. And they were gaining ground. He fumbled for the wiper blades and pulled himself back against the screen.

'Now I only see you!' yelled the driver.

Jed tried to peel himself back from the windscreen. But they were going too fast.

And he was pretty sure that even though the van hadn't stopped before, what lay ahead in the road was bound to stop them.

The rubbish lorry owned the centre of the road. It was travelling slowly. The bin men were working as if in a choreographed dance, rolling the waiting bins from the street, latching them to the back of the lorry, where they were lifted and emptied. They then pushed the bins back neatly into place as if they'd never been moved. It was almost like watching a ballet. One, Jed realised very quickly, that was about to be rather rudely interrupted.

The van mounted the curb for the second time and Jed used the momentum to fling himself back inside the cab and re-fix his seat-belt. The fastener clicked into place just as the van took out its first bin.

The bins toppled like tenpin-bowling balls. Rubbish cannoned up into the air in waves of stinking and rotten confetti. Bin men ducked and swerved as if they were skating on ice, the ballet transformed into a scene from a badly directed horror movie. And the windscreen, which moments before had been obscured by newsprint, was now awash with household waste, cabbage leaves and broken eggs.

Behind them the motorbikes wove through the debris like slalom skiers in the World Championships.

'I have a plan to lose them!' yelled the driver.

Jed wasn't sure how he stopped himself from laughing. 'You have a plan!' he bellowed.

The driver's eyes were wild and sparkling. He turned the steering wheel sharply to the left. Ahead of them was a wooden gate with the words 'Freizeitbad Salinarium' painted on it.

Jed had no idea what the driver's plan was. And he had no idea what the painted words meant. But neither of these things mattered as the fence shattered and splintered raining shards of wood around them and the van pushed forward.

'You have got to be kidding me!' yelped Kassia.

But the closeness of the motorbikes behind them was not a joke. And now they could see what the sign on the gate meant. The van was on the edge of an eight-lane outdoor swimming pool. And the driver obviously had absolutely no intention of stopping here either!

There was a narrow path round the side of the pool and a low wall marking the border. It was clearly not possible for the death wagon to drive on four wheels along the side as the wall was too close and the van wouldn't fit. But this didn't appear to deter the driver. 'Lean!' he yelled.

Jed presumed this was a German word he didn't understand but when he looked across at the driver, he saw he had pushed himself as far to the left as he could and was gesturing for Jed and Kassia to do the same. Then he rammed the van forward, purposefully clipping the curb at the beginning of the wall with the left wheels of the van.

It took a moment for Jed to work out what he was trying to do.

The man was insane. He was going to do a sideways wheelie in a death wagon beside an open-air Olympic-sized swimming pool!

But somehow the thrust of the engine, the angle of the curb and the weight inside the van propelled the vehicle on to two wheels. It rolled heavily to one side, and the wheels on Jed's side of the van bounced down on the top of the low wall edging the path. The driver gripped tight to the steering wheel. One wrong move here and the wheelie-ing van would ground on the wall or crash into the water.

From his raised position, Jed could see the drop below him. He held his breath. He closed his eyes. And the van slid forward, slicing along the narrow pathway with Jed, Kassia and the driver hovering above the open water.

There was a second when the van wobbled.

The momentum swung the van just a fraction to the side.

Jed braced himself for impact. To be engulfed in water yet again. But the water didn't come.

When the wheels bounced back on to level ground the pool was behind them. They were safe.

Sadly, not so safe were the sunbathers and picnickers who were spread across the open grass at the end of the pool.

Jed peered through the remnants of cabbage leaves and egg yolks on the windscreen as swim-suited holiday makers, and workers taking a break from the office, scattered in front of them. Little children dropped ice creams; sun-worshippers scrambled to wrap themselves in towels; picnickers fumbled with plates of chicken legs and potato salad as the van carved a path through the middle of them. Behind them, grannies grabbed knitting; teenagers grabbed each other; and small children screamed as the motorbikes sped through the wake of discarded blankets and sun mats.

But it wasn't what was behind them that was worrying Jed most. Directly in front of them, and blocking the exit to the street, was the tangled yellow tubing of an enormous waterslide.

It was totally clear, even from metres away, that the swoop and structure of the slide meant it would be impossible for the van to get around it.

Behind them the bikes were gaining ground.

But the slide was wide. And the hang of the shoot was low.

The engines of the bike were revving loudly.

'I go for it!' yelled the driver.

This from a man who hadn't been deterred by speeding trains, roundabouts or temporary roadworks. But how was he going to *go for it* exactly? Did he intend to try and drive under the overhang of the huge yellow tubing?

Jed looked at Kassia in panic. 'It's too low!' he yelled.

But the bikes were closing in. It was this or be cornered by them and surrender.

The driver glanced across at Jed as if waiting for

confirmation. Jed shrugged. Then he braced himself.

The driver floored the accelerator. And the van pitched forwards, aiming directly for the huge yellow slide.

There was a moment when Jed thought they'd made it. The windscreen was filled with the yellow light reflecting from the underside of the slide. But then there was the sound of the crunching and mangling of metal. The van shuddered. And like the lid of a pilchard can, the top of the van began to rip back and separate from the carcass. The roof tore from position, and the now exposed edging of the sides of the van worked like serrated knife blades on the underside of the yellow slide. They cut deep into the plastic tubing, gouging an enormous hole. Water spewed down into the van, pummelling on to Jed and the others so they could barely breathe.

Jed tried to scream at the driver to keep moving, but his words were drowned by the gush and thunder of the falling water.

The driver's foot was still hard against the pedal. The van edged forward, slicing free of the yellow tubing. There was a thud and banging from inside the back of the van. It was soon clear that the gaping hole on the bottom of the slide had not just deluged water down on them.

The screaming from the back of the van was terrifying.

Jed squirmed round in his seat and peered through the partition. A middle-aged woman wearing a spotty swimsuit and a floral pink bathing hat and goggles had been dumped by the slide on to the trolley in the back of the van. And her screams were unrelenting.

'Get her out!' yelled the driver, thrusting the van into gear again and ploughing forward as water gushed down from the severed slide. The bikers skidded and slipped in the waterfall behind them, but were still on their tail.

The woman in the back of the van was totally hysterical.

'Get her and water out!' yelled the driver again.

'How?' begged Kassia, spluttering and coughing.

The driver pointed to a release button on the panel at Jed's side.

'Really?' Jed said nervously.

'You have to! Weight slow us down!'

Jed was pretty sure that the onslaught on the wheels and bodywork of the van was probably the real reason the van was driving a little slower but he didn't like to argue. Besides, water was sloshing everywhere and the pitch of the woman's screams had reached a crescendo. He pressed down hard on the door release button. The rear doors flung open and the water from the slide cascaded out too, carrying in its wake the trolley and the middle-aged slide rider. The wheels of the trolley hit the ground and the trolley careered forward into the path of the bikers, who tore off to the side, their wheels spinning.

But they were not to be stopped. And neither was the death wagon.

Jed braced himself as the van spluttered forward towards another fence. This one, too, shattered and splintered like matchsticks as the van made impact.

There was a burst of exhaust fumes, and with the rear doors swinging wildly like broken wings, the van was back on the open road.

And even though the middle-aged woman in the floral bathing hat was far behind them, the bikers were only metres away.

The path was now a single track. The town of Bad Dürkheim was slipping into the distance. And the motorbikes were gaining ground.

Wind whistled through the cab, tossing cabbage leaves and newspapers in a swirling vortex, visible now through the space where the roof had been peeled away. The rear doors clapped together, bouncing open and closed with every turn in the road. And the driver gripped tighter to the wheel. 'It's you they want,' he blurted, shouting to be heard over the roar of the wind.

'You think!' Jed roared back.

The road was narrowing, the driver scanning the edge for a turning. 'I mean. I drive on. You get out. Good plan!'

'Crazy plan!' yelled Jed, as the driver shifted the gears and turned the van hard right at what was little more than a turning on to a narrow dirt track. They'd entered some sort of woodland. There was no real road and the van was bouncing on the path, lurching and rolling to the side as the engine groaned under the strain.

'We make them think you still here,' yelled the driver, ducking as branches from a low hanging tree strained into the cab.

Jed pushed the branches away and pulled Kassia closer. He didn't care if she was embarrassed now. 'How?' he yelled desperately.

The driver turned the van to the left. The motorbikes were closing in, weaving through the trees with ease.

'I slow down.'

Jed liked this part of the plan.

'I turn sharp right. You open doors. And jump. They not see. I keep drive.'

The driver wanted to use the open passenger door

as a screen. Trick the bikers into following the van while Jed and Kassia escaped.

The van hit a tree root. It rocked to the side. The engine squealed. Water sloshed in the footwell of the cab. The roar of the motorbikes was getting louder. They were streaking through the trees. Time was running out.

'Ready?' yelled the driver.

Jed was nowhere near ready. But the bikes were getting nearer. The van was struggling on the unmade road. If the plan was to work, then they had to do it now.

Jed looked across at Kassia. 'You can do this!' he said, not sure if it was a confirmation or a question.

Kassia's face showed only terror.

Jed unclipped his seat-belt and fumbled to release Kassia's. His hand hovered for a moment over hers. 'OK?'

Her answer was lost on the noise of the engine.

'The driver nodded and floored the accelerator one more time. 'You near Teufelsstein. Where you supposed to do the meeting!' He said. 'I think you find the devil.'

Jed had no time to work out what he meant.

The driver flung the gearstick forward, then yanked the steering wheel down hard right. Earth and dust plumed up in the air. The engine squealed and the van shuddered as it spun. Branches dragged through the cab. Birds scattered, squawking and screeching.

'NOW!' the driver screamed, his foot hovering for just a moment over the brake pedal.

The van shuddered. The air crackled with engine fumes. Jed opened his door and flung it wide. Then he grabbed Kassia's hand. They jumped. And the ground came up to meet them with a sickening thud.

The air punched out of Jed's lungs. Dark spots spiralled in front of his eyes. Beside him, Kassia groaned.

He reached for her arm, scared to speak; as if using his voice would give their location away.

The sound of the death wagon was thinning. The motorbike engines were still loud enough to be close to them, though. Jed didn't lift his head.

A motorbike slowed.

Jed's heart was in his mouth. He pressed his body down harder into the ground, fighting the fear that the pressure would shatter his ribs.

He waited.

He could hear Kassia's breathing beside him. The motorbike engine thrummed. The wheels churned leaves and clipped bracken.

They were going to be found.

It was over.

Then a shout. In German. Through the trees.

The engines revved sharply.

And the motorbikes raced away.

The air was still.

Jed wasn't sure how long he lay there without moving. Minutes. Maybe hours.

Then, finally, he lifted his head. Kassia rolled on to her side and looked up at him. They were so close that their breath mingled and suddenly it felt wrong to be so near to her. 'Are you OK?' he blurted, scrabbling to sit up.

Kassia pushed her weight down on her elbows. Then she laughed.

'OK. OK. Stupid question, I know.'

Kassia kept on laughing and then she doubled over and blew out a long breath.

'I meant apart from the near drowning, high-speed car chase and jump into bushes from a moving vehicle, *obviously*. Apart from all *that*, is your day going well?'

She rubbed her hand across her chest and smiled at him.

He leant towards her and reached for a cabbage leaf tangled in her hair. She watched him for a second longer than was comfortable and then looked down at the ground.

Results for river boy dea

Top / **All**

**Konspirieren Netzwerk** @konspirierenDE  4m
Ich glaube. #RiverBoyDeath #Neckar

**Meredith White** @merrymere  4m
I saw it all!! **#RiverBoyDeath** #Germany #holiday #witness

View Conversation

**NOAH** @NOAH  5m
**#RiverBoyDeath** ! _.. ·1+9

Fox @madmadmadmax  6m
·y terrible story. #loss #awareness **#RiverBoyDeath**

View Conversation

·sten @austentacious  6m
·e the plot for a film, this does

View Conversation

·lard @standardnews  6m
·rowns in Germany. #Riv

'The motorbikes,' she said quietly. 'Definitely NOAH?'

'Who else would want to chase a mortuary van?'

'But they can't know yet, can they? About us not really being dead?'

'Can't see how. We've just got to hope they only wanted to see the bodies.'

'And when there are no bodies?'

'Yeah. Well.' Jed didn't want to think about that. 'Least we won't be there for the big reveal. And there's a chance that driver lost them. We have to hang on to that.' He tried to look encouraging but he was pretty sure the conviction didn't reach his eyes. 'So? Any plans for the rest of the day?' he said in a voice he hoped sounded jokey.

She pulled her knees up towards her chest. 'This is Teufelsstein, yes?'

'So our lovely driver said.'

'I guess we find somewhere to wait for Dante and Jacob then.'

'Sure,' he said, jumping up and wiping the woodland debris from his trousers. 'Let's try and find somewhere quiet.'

Jed and Kassia had found a small clearing in the woods. There was a sign, tacked to a tree, with the word

'Teufelsstein' carved on it. So Kassia wanted to wait here. It was damp. It was getting dark. And the bark of the tree they were leaning against was digging into Jed's shoulders.

'They will come,' Kassia said again, rubbing her hands together. '*Dante* will come,' she said with even more conviction.

'I know. I know.' They'd been passing the same phrases backwards and forwards like shots in a tennis match for ages now, and with each utterance, Jed was getting less and less certain. Kassia would barely look at him. Her belief in her brother and her social worker was absolute. Jed was feeling less and less sure.

Jed wanted to talk about the possibility that something had happened. Something beyond Jacob and Dante's control that had kept them from reaching the meeting place. But he couldn't bear to voice the words aloud. Besides, Jacob and Dante not having found them yet wasn't the only thing he was worried about. His mind was churning thoughts, like the motorbikes had churned leaves as they'd raced through the woodland. And nothing he could do would shake the thoughts away.

'You're shivering,' Jed said gently to Kassia. 'Here. Take my jumper.'

'But you're shivering too.'

'It's not because of the cold.'

She said nothing as he wrapped the jumper around her shoulders, but pulled it tight, fiddling with the cuff of the sleeve.

'I'm so sorry,' he said at last, the words burning in the back of his throat. Everything was a mess. He sank his head into his hands, trying again to order the thoughts that were roiling there. Behind the pressure of his palms, the image of the dragon circled and spun.

'Hey, come on, Fulcanelli. Cheer up! They will be here. And we didn't die!'

He didn't lift his head from his hands.

'You don't like it when I call you that?'

He took his hands away from his face and rested them in his lap. 'I still can't get my head round it, that I'm some guy from the 1920s. It's too weird.'

'We've been over this. Not weird.' She hesitated a fraction too long. 'Well, OK. A little weird. But wonderful. And at least we know it's true now,' she added. 'The poison didn't kill you. The river didn't drown you. We can be sure. Fulcanelli the great alchemist,' she said with a flourish. 'It's who you are.'

That's what Jed was worried about. He looked at the creases in his palm. One line ran completely from one side to the other, totally unbroken. He wrapped his arms around himself as if he was doing the best he could to hold himself together. It meant he could no longer see the line on his hand. 'Can I ask you something?' he said quietly.

'Sure.'

'Do you think I should have done it?'

She arched one eyebrow. 'Jumped from the death wagon? Well it had been at least a couple of hours since we'd had a face to face battle with NOAH and so maybe fronting it out and—'

'Not jumping. I mean, taking the elixir.'

She paused. 'You're asking me if you should have drunk something that messed with your system and took you back to being seventeen and made it possible to live forever?'

'Yeah.'

She hit him playfully on the arm. 'Well if you hadn't done, none of this would have happened.'

He winced.

'Hey, come on, I'm joking.'

He was pretty sure it wasn't funny.

'Of course you should have made the elixir. It's incredible. It's wonderful. It's what everyone in the world wants to do, isn't it? Stop death.' Her eyes were sparkling. 'People are trying to do it all the time. Doctors, paramedics. Look what happened to me.' She touched nervously at the welts at the base of her neck where the paramedic had attached electrical paddles to restart her heart. 'Do you think the medics should have let me die?'

'No. Of course not!' How could she believe for a second he thought that! 'It's just, finding a way to live *for ever* is different. Isn't that playing God?'

'Well if it is, then you won!' She turned so she was fully facing him, the light of the moon framing her face. 'If life's a game then there are bad people out there. Bad things. Death being the baddest of all. And what you did was phenomenal and . . .' she searched for the best word she could. '*Good*. You are a good person, Jed. I believe you were good in the past when you were cooking up the elixir and you are good now. You need to remember that.'

But it was perhaps what he was remembering that was making her instruction so impossibly difficult.

'Supposing something has happened to Dante and Jacob,' he said at last.

Now it was obviously her turn to be scared. 'They will come,' she said defiantly. And then she turned so that her back was towards him and peered resolutely out into the gathering gloom.

# DAY 58

## 26th April

The first light of morning was breaking through the leaves. Jed had slumped against the tree, his arm, fallen in his sleep, was around Kassia's shoulder. Her head was resting on his chest. He stared down at her for a moment as the light glistened in her hair and danced across her cheek.

She opened her eyes and there was a moment of recognition before she pulled herself away and jumped up to stand beside him. 'What time is it? Where are they? Did they come?'

Jed fiddled in his pocket for the silver watch and snapped it open. The watch face was still misty from the traces of river water but the time ticked on relentlessly. 'Nearly seven,' he said.

Kassia pulled her phone from her pocket and shook it despondently. Unlike the watch, the phone hadn't worked since the river. Any way of making contact with her brother was gone, but Jed could see from the resolve on her face that Kassia's trust in him was still unwavering.

Jed's stomach rumbled. 'Should I go and try and get us some food?'

'No!' her answer was emphatic. 'I mean. It's OK. I'm not hungry.'

This seemed unlikely to be true, but two things were clear. Kassia was not ready to leave the meeting place. And she wasn't ready for Jed to leave either.

He stood for a while and watched as she paced backwards and forwards, lifting leaves with her feet. He took a twig and snapped it in half. There was a core of green running through the centre. But the twig looked old and gnarled on the outside. Appearances could be deceptive.

Jed tossed the twig into the undergrowth.

There was a rustling noise.

Jed stood up slowly, his back against the tree. 'Kass,' he hissed gently. She stopped walking.

Jed nodded towards the bushes and then, with one hand, he gestured to the left, pointing out the path they should make for when they ran. He reached his other hand out to pull her with him. Just as he lifted his foot to launch into a sprint, she broke away from him.

'I knew you'd come!'

Dante was pushing his way out of the undergrowth. He grabbed for Kassia, his eyes wild. He made no signs because his hands were wrapped around her but his eyes said everything he would have needed words for.

Kassia pulled herself out of his embrace to look at him. 'I'm OK. I'm OK.'

He hugged her again and then pushed her back so his hands were free to sign. 'I've been so worried. I thought I'd never find you!'

'I'm OK!' she said again, adding signs to her words this time. 'We both are. Where's Jacob?'

'In a minute. Let me look at you!' His eyes strayed to the welts at the base of her neck.

She fumbled awkwardly with the buttons of her shirt. 'It's all right. I have a strong heart.'

Dante was angry. 'I should never have let you out of my sight!'

'It doesn't matter. Jed saved me.'

Dante looked across and Jed wasn't entirely sure that the look was one of uncomplicated gratitude. There was a trace of anger there. And something which looked a bit like guilt. But Kassia was tugging Dante's arm to make him turn back to face her.

'Jed rescued me. NOAH wanted to prove he was Fulcanelli. They made him drink poison.'

The story was a little muddled. Kassia wasn't making it clear that the poison had been intended for Kassia and that Jed had chosen to drink it in her place. But Dante was impressed none the less.

'You did that!' he signed elaborately.

'Turns out I really am the Fulcanelli,' Jed signed awkwardly. 'No doubts there any more.'

Dante's face had softened a little and the anger seemed to have ebbed away. 'So it's true then. You really are a walking, talking immortal.'

Jed looked across at Kassia awkwardly. 'Yeah. Seems there's a bit of a problem with that actually.'

'Go on.'

'Turns out the elixir of life has to be taken six times to make the immortal bit permanent.'

'But you took it six times, right?'

'Maybe not.'

Dante shook his head. 'How d'you know?'

Jed wasn't entirely sure, and more importantly, even thinking about it to try and explain made fear bubble in his throat. The same emotion he'd seen hiding in Dante's eyes earlier pressed hard against his chest. 'The memory thing,' he signed slowly. 'When I see the flashbacks and the dates I think I took the elixir . . .' He hesitated for a moment and tried not to let his mind circle round the memories. 'There are always just five of them.'

'So you have to take it one more time?' queried Dante.

'Guess so.'

'And if you don't?'

'We're not sure,' cut in Kassia.

Jed took a deep breath. 'We *are* sure. But your sister doesn't like to face it.' He was trying to stop his signs from shaking but he was failing badly. 'No sixth dose and it's over. The immortality thing gone. I die.'

Dante looked uncomfortable but he did not look away. 'So you take a sixth dose then.'

Jed smiled at his conviction. 'There's a bit of an issue with that too.'

Dante's signs melted away and he didn't have to shape his fingers into words to communicate that he wanted Jed to go on.

'We reckon there's a time limit.'

Dante looked across at Kassia before turning back to Jed. 'How long?'

'About nine months.' Jed's fingers fumbled as he finished the last sign.

Dante obviously had no idea what to say in answer. He looked down at the ground, his hands still, no words wrestling to be free of his fingers.

Kassia looked round awkwardly and then stamped her foot hard on the ground in Dante's eyeline to get his attention and force him to look up and face her.

'We have nine months and that's for ever,' she said as if that was the end of the discussion. 'So where's Jacob?'

Dante's hands were still frozen.

Kassia stamped her foot again. 'You said he'd be here in a minute.'

'No.' His eyes would not look at her. Instead they focused down on the signs he was making falteringly with his hands. 'I said, I'd tell you in a minute.'

'Tell us what?'

Dante ran his fingers through his hair and began to pace as he tried to answer. 'I'm not sure what happened.'

Jed stepped forward and stopped Dante in his tracks. 'Where's Jacob, mate? You're scaring us.'

'I don't know.' Dante's face was drained of colour. 'We were at the B and B and we were going frantic. Then the call came from this Charlie guy at the hospital. Told us about the river.' He reached his hand towards the welts on Kassia's neck, as if the thought of what could have happened to her was so painful that just for a second he needed to take a pause from talking. 'Charlie told us the press would report that you'd drowned,' he went on at last. 'And Jacob kind of panicked. Said if the story reached Mum or Nat it would kill them.'

Jed looked across at Kassia and he could see that this thought hadn't occurred to her. They'd been so wrapped up in what happened that they hadn't had a chance to think about those at home in London.

Dante's hands were moving again. 'So we agreed that Jacob would go into town. He'd find a public phone and make the call. He didn't want anything traceable to his phone or where we were staying, you see. We thought that was safest.'

'So he rang Mum,' Kassia asked nervously. 'What did she say?'

'I don't know. Jacob never came back.'

Jed could see the anguish in his face, but Dante was determined to keep going with his explanation.

'I waited and waited. I had no idea what to do. He'd taken the car. All I kept thinking about was you being here. And I couldn't stand it. So I left. I took a bus to town and walked here.' His signs were starting to fragment.

'It's OK,' said Kassia. 'You had no choice.'

'There's always a choice, Kass. And I couldn't leave you here. But something bad must have happened.'

Jed spelled out the letters to form the word with his hands he knew both the others were thinking. 'NOAH?'

'They've got eyes everywhere,' confirmed Kassia. 'They must have followed Jacob.'

Jed tried not to think about the cage NOAH had held him in back in London. He tried not to let his mind imagine what NOAH would be doing to Jacob if they'd caught him. 'So we find him.' He tried to sound more confident than he was. 'The three of us together.'

'But where on earth do we start looking?' said Dante, who'd clearly given the problem lots of thought on his way to meet them. 'If NOAH have taken Jacob, he could be absolutely anywhere by now.'

They had no idea where they were heading, but somehow it seemed important to keep moving. Dante passed them squares of a rather crumbled cereal bar and Kassia's story about not being hungry was exposed immediately for the lie it obviously was. Jed smiled as she wolfed it down and held her hand out to her brother for more. 'What?' she said jokily. 'It's fruit and nut. Part of my five a day.'

Jed nodded and swallowed his own gratefully.

There was no real path to follow but they aimed

uphill. There seemed to be the unspoken agreement that they'd see more from here.

Jed's mind flitted back to the driver of the death wagon saying Teufelsstein was a beauty spot. The driver had obviously thought this idea a funny one but as Jed and the others made their way through the trees, he wasn't really sure why. The area was wooded. Flowers grew. Birds sang.

It was when the trees began to thin and the air grew cold that Jed began to think the driver might have had a point.

They'd entered some sort of clearing. The trees that edged the space were thin and spindly as if there were no nutrients in the soil to nourish them properly. The ground was blackened. It was clear nothing grew here, or if anything had, it had died and rotted down to nothing.

Suddenly Jed stopped walking. 'What's that?' he asked slowly.

In the shadow of the few spindly trees that remained was a huge rock. It was at least the height of two fully grown men, maybe taller, and as wide as a bus, the surface made shiny by years of weathering and rain. The edges were sharp and jagged and it was just possible to see that holes like steps had been worn or cut into the side. As they got closer, they could see a

41

sort of trough had been chiselled out of the flattened surface at the top of the steps.

'It looks like some sort of altar,' said Kassia nervously.

The air was even more chilly. The birds silent now. Jed noticed his breath was forming mist clouds on the air.

And then he noticed something else.

There was a man lying in the gulley on top of the rock.

The man was totally still. No misty breath was escaping his lips.

Jed and Dante hurried forward.

But Kassia stood where she was. Then she started to scream.

The unmoving man was Jacob.

'What have they done to him?' Kassia could barely form the words as Jed clambered up the face of the rock, scrambling to latch on to the footholds. The surface was hot, as if it was being heated from inside. Jed's fingers scorched. He struggled to keep from pulling his hand away, biting his lip to choke back the pain. His head felt too heavy for his own body and it was difficult to focus. When he blinked to clear his vision, he was staring down into Jacob's eyes. They were the colour of deep, dark pools of oil.

'Be careful with him,' Kassia yelled.

Dante scrambled up the rock too and crouched down. Jacob's body was sprawled between them. Dante didn't seem to have struggled at all with the climb and his own eyes were full of urgency as he slid his arm under Jacob's torso, begging Jed silently to help him.

Jed tried to stop his hands from shaking as, together, he and Dante began to lower Jacob's body down to the ground. At one point, Jacob seemed to hang suspended between them. Jed's grasp slipped.

'Don't let him fall,' screamed Kassia, running to join them as they manoeuvred Jacob tentatively round and propped him in a slumped seated position, his back against the stone altar. Jed fought to steady his own breathing as air caught painfully in his throat but the other two didn't seem to notice his discomfort. All eyes were on Jacob.

Jacob's own eyes were closed.

Kassia pressed her hands against her mouth. She said his name and it fell strangled from her lips. 'Jacob?'

His eyelids flickered.

Jed let out a breath of relief. Jacob was alive but how badly hurt he was, it was impossible to tell.

'What did they do to you?' Kassia asked falteringly.

Jacob turned his head awkwardly and stared at

each of them as if for a moment he didn't know who they were.

Kassia grabbed for his hand. 'Jacob. It's us.'

Jacob pulled away as if that arm was hurting, and Jed noticed a bulge of padding under the sleeve of his shirt. NOAH had beaten him then, but they'd taken the time to dress his wound.

Jacob was blinking as if waking from a long sleep. His eyes began to focus and something more than relief flickered there for a moment. Something darker, which he seemed to drive away with a shake of his head.

'What did they do to you?' Kassia begged again.

'I'm OK.' Jacob's voice was as thin as tissue.

Dante was waving his hands frantically, but the signs were muddled and confused. Jacob suddenly reached out and grabbed Dante's hands to silence them.

Kassia's torrent of questions couldn't be stopped though. 'Where did they take you? How did they hurt you?'

Jacob's eyes flitted from one face to another, the answers obviously too painful to put into words. It had taken Jed ages to be able to talk about the cage NOAH had imprisoned him in back in London. He knew Jacob wanted the questions to stop but Kassia was relentless.

'How did you get here?' she pressed.

This was the part Jed was struggling with most.

'Are NOAH still here?' Kassia shot her gaze to all the bushes and trees on the perimeter of the clearing.

'It's all right,' stuttered Jacob. His eyes darkened again. 'They've gone.'

'You sure?' Kassia was scanning the distant treeline. 'They just left you here? Do they realise we're not dead? Have they worked out about the river? Do they know you were meeting us here?'

Jacob lurched forward as if he'd been burned by the heat of the rock behind him or stabbed in the back. His voice was ragged and raw and Jed couldn't bear to look at him.

'I don't know how NOAH find out what they do,' Jacob stammered. 'Nothing is secret to them.'

Jed was pretty sure Jacob wasn't just answering the questions Kassia had been asking.

There was a moment of silence and when Jed finally turned, Jacob's voice was more metered and accompanied for the first time since they'd found him, with sign. 'NOAH have gone,' he said. 'People leave places for all sorts of reasons.'

Dante's look of horror was pitiful. 'I had to leave, mate,' his hands said awkwardly. 'My sister needed me.'

Jacob tapped Dante's hand gently with his own.

The bandage on his forearm wrinkled a little below his shirt and he winced. 'I get it. Family come first. Always. I get that.' He looked away. Kassia followed the direction of his gaze.

'You're sure NOAH aren't here,' she said again.

'I'm sure.'

But Jacob's answer didn't stop the surge of fear engulfing them as a crack sounded in the undergrowth at the edge of the clearing.

They were no longer alone.

Jed flung his arm round Kassia and pulled her spread-eagled to the ground beside him. He waited for the pain of the gun shot to come; for the bullet to drill into his shoulder blades. He waited for the darkness. Nothing.

Then a voice, light and airy drifted down from above them. '*Alles in Ordnung?*'

Jed turned and released Kassia. She shook herself as he unpinned her from the ground, blushing as she dusted soil from her arms.

'English then?' The stranger who'd appeared from the treeline was speaking again, this time more slowly. It was clear now, from the uniform he wore, that he was some sort of park warden. 'You OK? You looking like the feared. Guess broken twig shocked you?'

Jed mumbled an answer to hide his embarrassment.

Gun shot. Broken twig. It was an easy confusion. Could have happened to anyone. Well, anyone who knew a crazy scientific organisation was out to get them. 'We're fine. Thank you.' He wasn't really sure if that was true but it seemed like the only possible thing to say.

'You've been making with the acquaintance of the devil, have you?'

Jed felt his stomach turn to water. Did this park ranger *know* about NOAH and how they kidnapped people and tried to kill them?

'We are very proud of our Teufelsstein.'

It seemed that the warden was not talking about NOAH after all.

Almost as if to confirm this, he moved to run his hand along the rock behind them. His hand danced for a moment in each of the five holes cut into the surface. The rock didn't appear to be burning him like it had done Jed. But the warden's eyes were full of deep respect and maybe even reverence. 'It's a story stone,' he said at last.

Jed's mind was just about catching up with his heart rate and it seemed sensible to keep the warden talking. 'What's a story stone?' he asked.

The warden looked incredulous, allowing his finger to hover just a little longer over the highest hole cut into the rock. 'Story stones all the world over,' he began. 'Hiding places of important stories. You do the looking close to read them.' He considered for a moment before continuing in his explanation. 'Stonehenge in England,' he said excitedly. 'Tells story of time and man. Fight for control.' He made his hands into fists and acted out a mock boxing match as if man was really fighting time in some sort of game.

'And this stone?' cut in Kassia, in what Jed realised was a feeble attempt to divert attention away from the issue of controlling time. 'What's the story here?'

The warden ran his hand back across the first foothole. 'Where beginning?' he said ponderously. 'See five steps,' he waved towards each one. 'Now see bowl.' He pointed to the hollow dip at the top of the stone where they had found Jacob lying. 'Animals sacrificed here.' He ran his finger down a shallow groove gouged into the stone and leading from the hollowed dip. 'Blood runs away like so.'

Jed was not liking this story much.

But the warden was enjoying the effect he was having on his audience. 'Story says, maybe steps made by Devil's feet and tail when he rested here.' He began to walk around the stone as if it was a beast waiting, ready to pounce on its prey. 'See carvings now. Sunwheels. Runes. A skull, look. People add to stone story. Once symbol of man and woman here. But they have been, how you say?'

'Eroded?' offered Kassia.

'Died maybe,' said the warden. 'This stone book of death, see.'

'There are other kinds?' asked Jed.

'Of course. Stone books of life much more nice.' He smiled. 'Reading stone books of life lead to greater reward than scare in woods. If you read story stones of life, perhaps you fight death and win.' He moved his hands like a boxer again, striking the air with an elaborate final punch.

Suddenly the conversation was getting really interesting. 'Who believed that?' pressed Jed, desperate to know more but anxious not to scare the warden off.

But the man was on a roll, obviously eager to share. 'Alchemists,' said the warden. 'You heard of them?'

'Oh, we've heard of them,' said Jed painfully.

'Some say alchemists hid recipe for eternal life in books of stone.'

'So where would people find those?' urged Jed.

'You not so like our stone of death then?' grinned the warden. 'Shame. We think worthy of great respect.'

'It's a lovely stone,' reassured Kassia, obviously just as keen as Jed to keep the stranger talking. 'Well not lovely with all the death and blood and devil stuff, but . . .' She abandoned her attempts to appease the man. 'We'd just like to know about the stones of life. And where they are. Exactly.'

'All the world over,' laughed the warden. 'France. England. Czech Republic.'

'Oh, but you can be more precise, surely. About the alchemy ones. And the recipe for eternal life.'

The warden looked thoughtful. 'Prague,' he said sharply.

'Excuse me?'

'Prague. If not death you like, then Prague has the story stones of life.'

'I say we try Prague.' Jacob's voice was cracking slightly but Jed could see the determination in his face.

'No,' Jed was surprised by the strength of his own voice. 'We need to get you rested. Give you time to recover from what NOAH did to you.'

Jacob was limping through the trees, following the directions the warden had given them to the train station. 'I'm fine,' Jacob said with more conviction this time. 'I'm back now and we just need to forget about NOAH.'

'Forget about NOAH!' blurted Kassia, stumbling to keep up.

Jacob turned. 'I didn't mean that. Not forget about

them. Just about what they did to me.' He scuffed his feet through the leaves. 'Forgetting about NOAH is actually the last thing we should do. We need to get out of Germany quick.'

'But Prague?' Jed clarified. 'Because some woodman with an obsession with the Devil's Stone seems to think it's a good idea.'

Jacob winced and looked away.

'Aren't we clutching at straws?' Jed added.

'Straws are all we have,' said Jacob. 'And my job was to help you find answers and to keep you safe. At the moment I don't seem to have done a very good job of either of those things. So I say, let me get this mission back on track.' He nodded towards Jed and his eyes flickered with something that looked like pain. 'Dante's just told me about how you have nine months to find the elixir. So I don't think we have time to waste.'

It was Jed's turn to look down at the ground and scuff his feet through the leaves.

'Prague was a centre for alchemy,' Jacob pressed on with his argument. 'That came up when Dante and I were talking to the guy in the alchemy museum in Heidelberg castle.'

'Yeah. And going to Heidelberg turned out so well!' said Jed.

'Point taken, but you made sense of the year limit because of what you found out at the castle. And you found out about the sixth doses.'

'But books of stone?' said Jed without conviction. 'Really?'

Jacob was beginning to look desperate. 'You tell me you didn't work stuff out by reading stones and buildings. St Paul's Cathedral – that gave you the idea of the year in the first place, didn't it? And the O2 and the tower at Heidelberg just confirmed it. If I'm wrong, then tell me and we'll go somewhere else.'

Jed had slowed down. He was trying to make sense of all that Jacob had said.

'Tell me I'm wrong, Jed.'

'I don't think you're wrong.' He didn't look up but rubbed his hands together. 'It's just . . .' He hesitated. 'I know we need answers and I want them more than I can even begin to tell you all. But when I touched the Devil's Stone it was hot. Kind of fiery like a warning.'

Jacob steadied himself against a tree. He ran his finger inside the neck of his shirt.

Jed felt a wave of guilt about returning the conversation to the place Jacob was obviously trying so hard to forget. 'I'm sorry.'

Jacob didn't answer.

'It's just this is all too weird, isn't it?' said Jed

looking for reassurance across at Kassia and Dante.

'Too weird for words,' signed Dante, playfully throwing his hands apart as if he could no longer sign. 'But weird is what we do, Jed,' he signed slowly, bringing his hands back together. 'It's kind of what we are.'

Jed blew out a breath and looked across the trees to where the train track carved its way into the distance. He tried to smile. 'I can't think of anywhere else to go and I agree with you. We've kind of done Germany for a while.'

'Prague it is then,' Jacob said purposefully. 'What have we got to lose?'

Jed knew the answer. But he said nothing. He pushed his hands deep into his pockets and followed Jacob towards the road that would take them to the station.

# LES DEMEURES
# PHILOSOPHALES

FULCANELLI

Préface de E. Canseliet F. C.

DES CATHÉDRALES

ET L'INTERPRÉTATION ÉSOTÉRIQUE
DES SYMBOLES HERMÉTIQUES
DU GRAND-OEUVRE

PRÉFACE DE E. CANSELIET, F.C.H.

Ouvrage illustré de trente-six planches
d'après les dessins de
JULIEN CHAMPAGNE

PARIS

BETRACHTUNG

FRANZ KAFKA

## Works [edit]

...e two books by Fulcanelli are

...Le Mystère des Cathédrales (The Mystery of the Cathedrals), written during 1922 and published in Paris during 1...[21]

...Les Demeures Philosophales (Dwellings of the Philosophers), published in Paris during 1929.[21]

...The books are written in a cryptic and erudite manner, replete with Latin and Greek puns, alchemical symbolism, do...
ignorant.

A third book, Finis Gloriae Mundi (End of the World's Glory),[22] was also reportedly being prepared for publication...
the timing for publication of the book was not right and so it was never in fact published. However, a book by the...
shown to be a counterfeit.[23]

## ...ulture [edit]

Scott Mariani deals with the subject of the alchemist's...
...chemist.[25] ...ajor theme o...

# DAY 59
## 27th April

'My god, is that some sort of gun?' Victor Sinclair stood in the doorway of Cole Carter's hotel bedroom. Cole was bending over a desk littered with what looked like bottles of ink. He held something silver in his hand. It was shaped like a revolver.

Cole sniffed sneeringly. 'You read too much, kid.'

'Is that a gun?' Victor pleaded again.

Cole stood up straight. He held out his hand, his eyes glinting. 'Yeah, it's a gun. But not the sort you're thinking. It's a tattoo gun, you idiot. What do you think I am?'

Victor wasn't sure how to answer that question. He'd spent hours with Carter now and he had no sense that he knew anything about him at all. Except that the guy obviously used a ton of products on his hair to keep it greased back so firmly. And that he rarely took

56

his leather coat off. In fact Victor was pretty sure he'd never seen the man without it.

'What do you need a tattoo gun for?'

Cole smiled. 'Well not for you, yet.' He put the gun back on the table and the ink bottles wobbled. 'You have to earn the mark.'

Victor didn't really understand what Carter was on about, but he hadn't come here to chat about tattoos. 'I need to talk to you,' he said.

'I'm not your mother, kid. You got love problems you need to have a word with her.'

'My mother's dead,' snapped Victor. 'My dad too and my sister. I'm pretty sure you know all the details.'

Carter folded his arms. 'Kind of goes with the territory of being a worker at NOAH,' he said. 'Loss of family and all that.'

'Yeah well. I don't want to talk about my family.' This wasn't entirely true. Victor did want to talk about them. He wanted to know exactly what work his dad had been involved in and what NOAH was all about. But that wasn't the issue that was eating him up inside at the moment. 'I need to talk about the girl in the water,' he blurted.

'You had the hots for her?'

Please, could this idiot be any less sensitive. 'No,

I did not have the hots for her. But . . . what happened . . . I can't get it out of my mind. The ropes and them jumping and . . . We killed her, Carter.'

'We didn't kill her. She jumped into that river.'

'Because of us!'

Cole stepped forward, pulled Victor into the bedroom and slammed the door. 'Keep your voice down, kid. You want the whole hotel to know?'

'I'm sorry. It's just I can't get the image out of my head. Their bodies covered over and . . .'

'Yeah, well. These things happen.'

Victor recoiled. 'Are you for real?'

Cole's forehead was folded into deep lines. 'You knew what you were getting involved in when you joined up.'

Victor grabbed Cole's arm. 'But that's the point! I've no idea what I'm involved in. I didn't sign up to see people get killed.'

'But you did sign up.'

'Well sort of. I signed papers to get me out of that hell-hole care home I was living in and to move into a place my dad had said should look after me. But I didn't know we'd be chasing a kid who's supposed to live for ever and then watching people die. I didn't know we'd be doing what we did on that bridge and my mind keeps going over and over what I saw and—'

Cole held up his hand. 'You have to calm down, kid.'

Victor could feel something like tears burning in his eyes and nothing would make him cry in front of this man. But he was scared. Really scared. He'd thought NOAH was going to give him a home and keep him safe. He'd had no idea they would stop at nothing to get answers and he wasn't even really sure what questions they were asking.

Cole's face seemed to soften. 'Look, kid. This is big. Really big. You're involved in a chase for a guy who's going to live for ever and that chase isn't going to be pretty. There's going to be collateral damage along the way.'

Victor's stomach cramped. He was pretty sure he was going to throw up. 'She was just a teenager. And he wasn't the guy who's going to live for ever anyway. We got it wrong.'

Cole began to pace slowly in front of the desk. 'I wouldn't be so sure about that,' he said, tracing his finger along the tattoo gun. A droplet of ink seeped on to the tip of his finger. 'Seems we might have been closer to the truth than it seems.'

He stopped walking.

'You need to stop worrying and get yourself ready

for action. No one died in that river, kid. The chase is still on.'

Kassia knew that Jed was looking at her. He'd barely glanced out of the window during the journey to Prague and now they'd finally disembarked from the train, he was staring again. 'I'm OK,' she said at last.

'Sure?'

Where did she start? Did she tell him she was terrified? Did she explain that every time she moved, the welts across the base of her neck pulled and stretched so that she was back inside the ambulance fighting to stay alive? Did she tell him that in the silence, she listened to be sure her heart was going to beat again? Did she mention the flashbacks to the river and the water pressing down on her when everything she saw dissolved to inky black? And if she told him all that, should she tell him about how afraid she was that the answers they searched for wouldn't be in Prague at all?

But Prague was about the elixir. It was about him, not her.

'Of course I am. I'm fine. Really.'

She could tell he didn't believe her. He sank down on to the curb, his feet in the gutter. She sat down beside him.

Kassia tucked a loose strand of hair behind her ear. 'Nine months is ages,' she said, leaning forward to re-lace her trainers as a way of not making eye contact. 'That's like the whole, entire time it takes to have a baby. From when it's nothing bigger than an eyelash, to when it's a great, whopping, proper human.'

Jed wrinkled his face in confusion.

'Elephants are pregnant for twenty months so of course it would be great to have longer. But rabbits are only pregnant for a month so it could be so much worse.' She was rambling and even though she'd tied her shoelaces twice already, she undid them and tied them again.

'I think your trainers are OK,' he said quietly. 'Even if you're not.' He leaned forward and for a moment it looked like he was going to rest his hand on hers. But he thought better of it and folded his arms across his chest.

They sat in silence, watching the tourists and travellers pouring out of the station and into the city, and Kassia wondered how these people could be leading such ordinary lives when everything about what she and Jed needed to do was so extraordinary. How could these people not know? And just be living? How could any of them not be counting down the days and the minutes until life was no longer possible?

Suddenly, Kassia saw Jacob and Dante emerging from the crowd, carrying food. Jacob had said no more about what NOAH had done to him. He insisted that he was fine and had rejected every attempt they'd made to get him to talk about what had happened. So they were all pretending everything was OK. Just another layer of pretence that everything was normal.

'No idea what any of this tastes like,' said Jacob, passing over plastic bottles of something called *Kofola*, which Kassia presumed was some sort of cola. 'I think the guy at the counter said this stuff should give us energy, although I'm not really sure he understood what I was asking, so he might have told us this will give us stomach ache and make us ill for days.'

He passed Kassia a doughy, baked snack and she broke into it keenly.

'It's called *butchy povidly*,' added Jacob. 'Looked good to me. Some sort of chocolate croissant, I think.'

Kassia's stomach rumbled as if suddenly remembering she hadn't fed it anything more substantial than squares of crumbled cereal bar for hours. The *povidly* was delicious. The brown paste filling wasn't chocolate – more like some sort of plum jam – but it was comforting and filling, and washed down with the *Kofola* it certainly gave her an energy boost.

'So where now?' signed Dante, looking up at Jacob as traces of sugar spilled from his signing fingers.

They'd been forced to spend a night in Bad Dürkheim before the first train could take them out of Germany. Jacob had used this time to show them he was back in charge. He'd found a public phone and made the promised call to Anna and Nat to tell them that whatever they saw in the news, Kassia hadn't drowned in the River Neckar. Anna had freaked out but everyone had expected that. She demanded they come home. They'd expected that too. It didn't change Jacob's plans. Instead he'd used the PC in the hotel reception to print out tram timetables and Google routes to the Municipal Library. If there were stone books in Prague then this seemed like the best place to start looking for information about them.

Kassia could feel Jed staring at her again.

'It will be all right,' she said, and she wasn't sure if it was the effect of the plum jam and sugar or just that she was tired of feeling scared, but a tiny part of her dared to believe it.

And their sense of hope actually intensified when they reached the library.

A flight of wide marble stairs with shiny brass handrails stretched up from the street doorway to the main internal entrance. Kassia used a handrail as she climbed and tried to hide the fact that her breath caught in her throat with the effort of each step.

It was the structure at the top of the stairs that offered hope.

An enormous column sat right in the centre. It looked like a huge industrial chimney, the sort Kassia was used to seeing on old power stations like the one at Battersea on the banks of the River Thames. The tower was so wide that five or six people linking hands would have only just managed to encircle it. It was what the tower was made of, though, that was most intriguing. Books. They'd been laid flat and slotted together like interlocking bricks to form the sides of an enormous, rainbow coloured stronghold. In the front of the structure, shaped like a teardrop, but taller than an adult, was an opening that worked like a window. Kassia and Jed stood beside each other and peered inside, first down, and then up to where the ceiling should have been. But the tower extended through the floor and up towards the sky, no limit on the expanse of books. They went on for ever, as far as the eye could see. The yellowed pages turned inwards so the shaft glowed with an unearthly cream light.

'There're millions of them,' said Jed.

'There's an infinite number, actually,' said Jacob. 'According to the sign. But it's a trick. Done by mirrors at the top and bottom. The image reflected again and again so what you see seems unending.' He tapped Kassia on the shoulder. 'Come on. You shouldn't always trust everything you see.'

Kassia pulled away from the teardrop opening and her vision swam a little as her eyes adjusted to the proper perspective of the here and now.

Jed moved to scan the outside edging of the structure, stumbling a little before standing ramrod still.

'Jed?'

'Look!' His voice was breathy.

She *had* been looking. And the structure was impressive and everything but now they needed to get inside and find out about the stone books they'd come to see.

But Jed was not ready to turn away. He was pointing to a book, spine outwards, high in the lattice work of the tower. Kassia stepped back to the sculpture and stared up at the angle of his gaze. And her heart leapt into her mouth.

'You see it?' hissed Jed.

She couldn't form the word to answer but nodded her head vigorously.

'Did you know?'

This time she shook her head.

Jacob and Dante were getting impatient behind them. Dante stamped his foot, a not so subtle sign that they needed to get moving. But Jed was clearly not going anywhere until he'd made them see the name on the book he was pointing at.

'Fulcanelli,' he whispered.

'It could be anyone with the same name, right?' Dante signed frantically.

'Of course,' said Kassia, keen they didn't get too carried away with themselves. But Jed, initially so reluctant to leave the sculpture, was racing now towards the doors of the library.

People were milling about but Jed charged towards an information desk which curved in a semicircle just behind the main doors. A librarian was resting her chin in her hand and staring at a computer screen. 'Excuse me,' Jed whispered. 'Do you speak English?'

The librarian's face tightened as if Jed had just asked her if she was capable of breathing in and out. 'Better than your Czech, I'm guessing,' she said. 'You want to know about the sculpture?' she said.

'Erm. Yes. Sort of,' said Jed.

'Called Idiom. Made by Matej Kren. Moved here in 1998. There are—'

'Well, not the actual sculpture. But one of the books in it,' interrupted Jed, more loudly this time.

'There're a lot of books,' the librarian said dismissively.

'There's one by someone called Fulcanelli,' Jed blurted. 'Do you know anything about that book?'

'Sure.' The librarian took a deep breath. 'Fulcanelli was an alchemist. We're pretty big on alchemy round here, you know. Our links go back—'

'The book in the tower!' Jed interrupted again. 'Fulcanelli.'

The librarian pursed her lips in annoyance but she carried on with her explanation. 'Fulcanelli wrote three books. I think there's a copy of the second book in the sculpture too.'

'Just the first and second book?' pressed Jed. 'Not all three?'

The librarian seemed to find this question amusing. She began to type on the keyboard in front of her and watched as the screen filled with information. 'Yep. I'm right. It says here only two of Fulcanelli's books were published. *The Mystery of the Cathedrals* and *Dwellings of the Philosophers*. Odd really. They're supposed to be about alchemy but they go on about buildings.'

'And the third book?' Jed said, looking eagerly across at Kassia.

'There is no third book,' explained the librarian,

reading from the screen. 'Oh, look, there *is*. It was called *Finis Gloriae Mundi*. Says here that means *End of the World's Glory*. It was supposed to be Fulcanelli's *great work*.'

'But it's not in the tower? You don't have it here on the shelves?'

The librarian was getting a little exasperated. 'The third book wasn't published.' She jabbed the computer screen, marking out the section of information she needed to share. 'The book containing the *great work* was given to one of Fulcanelli's friends. There was this group called Brothers of Heliopolis.'

'Yes!' Jed was urging her to go on.

'And one of the brothers, called Eugène Canseliet, took the book.'

'And what did he do with it?'

The librarian looked down at the screen. 'According to this, he destroyed it.'

'What?' Kassia couldn't help herself from cutting in. 'Why would he do that?'

'Well I guess whatever was in the third book by Fulcanelli was even more boring than his ramblings about buildings in the first two,' quipped the librarian.

'Do you have them though? Here to borrow?' asked Jed. 'The first two books?'

'Sure. If you're members of Prague Municipal

Library. And if you're not, I'd need ID to make you members.'

Jed glanced across at Kassia.

'Maybe we could just look at them here, you know, not take them out on loan?' Kassia suggested.

The librarian sighed. Kassia wondered if she had targets about how many new members of the library she could sign up in a month. 'OK. Give me a moment. I'll see if I can find you copies.'

Jed nodded gratefully. 'Perfect.' He said, watching the librarian disappear behind the stacks. 'This *is* perfect, right?'

Kassia didn't want to say her fears out loud. But by the time the librarian had returned with two rather battered copies of the books by Fulcanelli, and the four of them had been shuffled towards a reading bay, she was finding it even more difficult to keep quiet.

'Anything?' she said as Jed flicked through the first book. 'Any connection?'

The earlier excitement in Jed's face was draining away. 'It's in Czech for a start,' he said despondently. 'But I thought there'd be something. You know, a trace of something I remembered. Maybe if we could track down the books in English.'

Kassia looked across at Dante and her brother lifted

his shoulders supportively as if encouraging her to say what she guessed he was thinking too. 'Jed. It's great about the books. But the recipe for the elixir's not going to be in them, is it?'

Jed slowed the pages under his fingers and stared at her.

'These books are in the public domain. Anyone can get hold of them. So, if they contained the recipe for eternal life, don't you think someone would have found it by now? Lots of people. NOAH even?'

Jed lowered his head but she kept on talking.

'The recipe won't be written in a book. It will be hidden. And all the clues before have come from symbols and buildings and . . .' she hesitated. 'And stones. That's what we're here for. Stones of life, with secret messages that only a few can read.'

Jed closed the book in front of him, his hand pressing down a little longer than was necessary on the cover to ensure that it stayed shut.

'It doesn't mean the hunt's over, Jed. Just that it's not going to be easy.'

'I just . . .'

'I know.'

Dante stepped forward. He was smiling a little too brightly. 'Let's go and ask your new friend about the books of stone,' he said with his hands. 'Messages might be difficult to read sometimes. But not impossible.'

It took about twenty minutes for the librarian to give them details. She was very proud of Prague's links with alchemy and yes, she knew all about the books of stone. After much persuading, she finally told them there was someone who might be able to explain the idea behind the stone books to them properly. That person could be found at the House of the Stone Ram.

Prague was thronging with people: tourists, backpackers and coach parties who stopped without warning to take photographs or angle selfie sticks skywards. Coloured houses hemmed them in and stretched four or five storeys towards the sky. Stone-work had been carved and moulded to form hanging branches and garlands strung above windows and doorways. In the spaces below the bright russet roofs, pictures had been made of stone and brightly painted to give each house and building its own unique decoration.

'The pictures are instead of street numbers,' signed Dante, who'd been given charge of the scribbled instructions from the librarian.

Kassia thought the system would make life confusing. But she had to admit that the painted pictures were fascinating.

Eventually they found a street called Celetna. There was a hotel on the corner, and next to that a small pavement café.

Dante came to a halt outside a tall white building. A large stone sculpture was sandwiched between the windows on the second and third floor. It was unpainted, its dark stone contrasting with the whitewashed walls that bordered it. It was of a large ram, his horn pointed towards the balconied window.

'Looks more like a unicorn than a lamb,' said Kassia, and she was sure that Jed flinched a little beside her as if she'd said something wrong.

At the street level of the building there were three huge, rounded archways, the central one being easily the widest. A thick wooden door spanned the arch. 'Who's going to do this?' asked Jacob.

'Me,' said Jed, before the others had even had time to think about a strategy.

There was no doorbell and as the entrance was back a little from the street, the sound of his knocking echoed as his clenched fist beat on the unpainted wood. There was no answer. He knocked again.

After the third knock, there was a grating noise, like metal being dragged across metal, and then a small square opening, cut into the huge wooden door at about head height, swung open.

A man's face peered out. Deep wrinkled lines circled his eyes and edged his mouth, and his neck sagged with folded skin, making it look like the trunk of a very old tree.

'We wonder if you could help us,' said Jed.

The man's watery blue eyes darted from left to right as if taking in the fact that Jed was not alone.

'We wanted to ask about the stone books of Prague.'

The blue eyes stilled. He moved his mouth as if he was about to speak. He scanned his eyes from left to right again, and then, accompanied by a sharp intake of breath, he pulled his face away from the opening and slammed it shut.

'Great,' snapped Jed. 'Absolutely fantastic!'

'Maybe we offended him,' suggested Kassia. 'Speaking in English, I mean. Perhaps we should try in Czech.'

She took the travel book Jacob had bought in the gift shop next to the library and scanned it for common phrases, practising the most appropriate one over and over in her head before raising her own hand and banging on the door.

She was just about to bang the wood for the fifth time when the small square opening flung open and the wrinkled face appeared again.

'*Můžete nám pomoci*,' Kassia said awkwardly.

'What do you want with the stone books?' the man snapped.

Kassia lowered the guidebook. Using English was obviously not the problem, then.

The man's nostrils flared. His eyes darted once again from left to right.

There was a second when he hesitated, as if his eyes had settled on Jed and he was unsure for a moment. But then, with double the speed and noise with which he'd done so the first time, he slammed the opening shut.

'What now?' yelped Jed, throwing his hands upwards as if he was hoping an answer would fall from the clouds.

'Goulash,' said Jacob.

It sounded to Kassia as if he was swearing in Czech. But then Jacob delved in his wallet to find some money and gestured towards the café to the right of them.

'Go and get something substantial to eat and I'll do what I can to get us inside,' Jacob added, passing Kassia some folded bank notes.

'You're going to break in?' signed Dante, his signs wide and incredulous.

Jacob batted Dante's hands still. 'Of course not. There's more than one way to get what you want in

74

life. Just give me time.'

Kassia thought at first Jed wouldn't leave with them. His shoulders were hunched defensively and it took her several attempts to lead him away. But Jacob seemed clear he wanted to do this alone and so, reluctantly, Jed joined her and Dante as they made their way to the café. A waitress led them to a table at the back and Kassia put in three orders for the house special.

The goulash, when it came, looked rather sloppy. But Kassia was ravenous so she plunged her spoon into the bowl and began to eat. The meat fell apart in her mouth, and the sauce was so hot it made her skin prickle. It was good. And comforting. She ate for a while before looking up from her bowl.

Jed was resting his own spoon in the goulash and tracing circles as the steam rose.

'You should eat,' signed Dante. 'Every chance we get mate, you should take it.'

'How does he think he's going to do it?' said Jed, resting the spoon on the side of the bowl so he could sign.

'Doesn't matter, does it, as long as he gets us inside,' said Kassia.

Jed didn't look too sure. 'He knows what he's doing, right?'

Kassia's spoon clanged against the side of the bowl. 'Jacob always knows what to do. Trust us, he's been our social worker for years. Even before dad died. He's always there for us. He's come halfway across Europe, at the drop of the hat, just to keep you safe.'

'I'm sorry,' said Jed. 'It's just we don't know how badly NOAH hurt him. I just wish he'd let us stay with him, you know.'

'You would have missed the feast,' signed Dante, before tearing a section of bread and dipping it into the goulash. He gulped it down, wiped his hands together and then continued to sign. 'We're all shattered, mate. But Jacob's a good guy and I think he's OK now. If anyone can get us into that house, then he can.'

Jed nodded, and sipped from his spoon. Kassia could see the heat flooding his body and his shoulders relaxing slightly.

She looked down at the table. A splash of goulash had dropped on to the spotless white cloth. Her mum would have said something about the stain but her mum was hundreds of miles away pretending her only daughter was dead. Kassia's heart felt sore and she was pretty sure that this time it had nothing to do with the electric shocks she'd been given by the defibrillator in the ambulance.

When she looked up, Jacob was standing at the head of the table. 'We're in,' he said. 'Follow me.'

From Montgomery's office in The Shard in London, Victor could see the river. The Thames curled at the foot of the building like an oily black snake. He'd read lots of books about London. He knew the Romans had chosen to build here because the tides from the sea reached no further than the city. He knew Parliament had to close once because of the stench of the sewage dumped into the water. And he knew there were forty-five locks along her route. This kind of proved, he thought, how men had to keep fighting to control her.

Victor turned away from the window. Looking at the river made him feel uneasy. Instead, he peered at the wall. It was papered with documents. Emails, receipts, phone transcripts, maps, photos, passports. There was not a space untouched. Overlapping edges curled upwards as if straining to be free, forced into place by map pins, connected with coloured thread. A flood of information made of ink.

In the centre, ringed as if trapped within the circling segments of the body of a snake, was one particular picture. A boy. Wild hair, bright eyes. Victor remembered how the boy had looked different when he'd seen him here. Locked inside a cage. He'd looked different too on the banks of the Neckar. His hair cut short; the red was patchily covered in black. But it was the same boy.

And everyone at NOAH seemed to believe that they knew who this boy was now.

Fulcanelli. A boy who would live forever.

Victor looked up quickly as a walking stick rapped against the floor. Montgomery was staring at him. 'Carter tells me you were feeling uncertain about things.'

Great. So that's why he'd been called straight to the office as soon as they were back in the UK. Carter had dropped him in it. 'I was just a bit shaken up by the stuff at the Neckar. That's all.'

Montgomery's cane clipped again on the white flooring tiles. 'But you're feeling more settled now?'

'Actually . . .' Victor didn't know where to start. 'I've been wondering. You know. About this. And me. And how I sort of fit, if you know what I mean?'

Montgomery raised one eyebrow. 'You want out? To go back to Etkin House?'

Victor was totally sure of his answer to the second question. But his response to the first had kept him awake all night.

Montgomery took a deep breath. 'Look, Victor, I know all this is hard for you. Landing in a world that's full of secrets and a history you don't really understand.' He pointed up at all the pictures and documents on the wall behind him. 'But we have a chance to find the boy who survived poison and drowning and all this.' He pointed up at a photo of a train crash and another of trees stripped bare by a hurricane. 'You've got to see how important this is.'

'But Cole said there would be more collateral damage. And I'm not sure I'm cool with that side of things.'

Montgomery ran his finger thoughtfully down a newspaper article showing a solar eclipse. 'This is a war, Victor. And there are always losses in war. And I can understand if this is all too much for you.' He took another deep breath. 'We can always make arrangements for you to terminate your agreement with us. If that's what you want.'

He glanced back and Victor tried to slow the racing of his heart. This was it then. His chance to get away. And that *was* what he wanted. He was nearly entirely sure and the words were burning on his tongue.

'I want to show you something,' cut in Montgomery before Victor had had a chance to speak. 'If you're going to be leaving us, I mean.' He reached up to the pinboard of pictures and took one that had been set a little to the left. It was old and dog-eared at the corner.

Black and white and rather smudged.

Victor took it. He expected to see another image of the Fulcanelli. This wasn't that.

'Your father,' said Montgomery in explanation. 'Years ago, you can tell. At the beginning of his journey with us.'

Victor couldn't take his eyes from the photo.

'It was taken just after he lost your mum and sister.'

Victor scanned the image. He had no photos of his dad at all. Etkin House hadn't gone a bundle on personal property.

'You can have that,' said Montgomery.

'Why was it on that board?' stuttered Victor.

'Because Department Nine is where he worked, Victor. This was his office. Some of these are his notes and findings on Fulcanelli. Go on. Take it. He'd want you to have it.'

Victor's mind flashed him back to his first meeting with Martha Quinn in the sitting room of Etkin House. 'Your father wanted you to be part of NOAH,' she'd said.

'I'll get things arranged,' said Montgomery quietly. 'Sort all the paperwork so you can—'

'I'll stay,' blurted Victor, sliding the photograph into his jeans pocket and leaving his hand pressed hard against it.

Montgomery smiled. 'I'm glad to hear that's what you want,' he said. 'But I'm afraid it's not possible for you to stay.'

Victor gripped tight to the photo. 'But I made a mistake. I don't want to leave. I was just—'

'You can't stay,' went on Montgomery, 'because we have a new lead. I need you and Carter to leave the country again.' He stepped closer to the wall of images and withdrew a pin. The end was tipped with a small red bead, glistening like a drop of blood. He pushed the pin hard into the waterway of images. The paper he pierced creased with the pressure and a tiny fold, like a scar, ran from the bead of blood down between the boy's eyes.

'How did you do it? What did you say?' pressed Jed, hurrying after Jacob as he led the way out of the café.

Dante thumped Jed's arm, his annoyance written across every line of his face. Jed had forgotten to sign but he'd been too keen to get answers. 'Sorry,' he mumbled, rubbing his fist in circles across his chest.

Out on the street, Jacob stopped and turned to face them. 'Said we were interested in alchemy. That we'd heard of the stone books. That we wanted as much information about the elixir of life as possible.'

Jed stood back a little. 'You didn't tell him about

me? You know, why we need to know?'

It was Jacob's turn to thump Jed now. 'Of course not. What d'you take me for?'

'And he's seriously going to help us?' said Kassia. 'He looked right grumpy before.'

'If we stop messing about out here, he will!' groaned Jacob. 'Come on.'

The main door to the House of the Stone Ram was open barely more than a crack. Jacob took the group inside. The old man nodded at them each in turn. He looked smaller close up, but his eyes were still as determined as they'd been before. There would be no messing with this man, that was obvious.

'Seriously. How did you persuade him?' hissed Jed. He had a really bad feeling about this.

Jacob didn't answer.

The old man strode ahead. He led them across a large open hallway with an elaborate sweeping staircase, to a small and rather battered door in the corner. Beyond the door was a flight of stairs that led sharply upwards. They were uncarpeted and the walls beside them bare, in stark contrast to the deep reds and golds of the decoration in the hall. These must be servants' stairs, Jed supposed, as he climbed.

They moved on for several flights and entered a low-ceilinged room that stretched the whole width of the building. In the far corner was a narrow rickety bed, draped in crocheted blankets and a patchwork quilt fraying at the seams.

The old man directed their gaze away from the sleeping area and instead waved his hand at chairs which ringed a large round table in the centre of the room. Jacob took the lead and sat down first. Jed hesitated. The lack of natural light unnerved him. He looked across at Kassia, then chose a seat closest to the head of the stairs, tapping the chair to his left so that she sat next to him. He pulled his chair closer to her.

'Andel has very kindly agreed to help us,' said Jacob, pointing to the old man and wrapping his explanation in sign for Dante's benefit.

Jed felt his heart thump. How much did this man know? Could they trust him? Had Jacob protected their secret with enough care?

'This house was used in the past as a testing place for new alchemists who came to work in the castle,' added Jacob. 'And so Andel here,' Jacob ploughed on, 'has agreed to test us, just like any seeker of the elixir of old.'

Testing? Worthiness? What had Jacob got them into?

All eyes looked towards the old man.

'You seek the recipe for the elixir of life,' he said

slowly as if allowing time for Kassia to convert his words into sign or perhaps for himself to translate from his own language into English before he spoke. 'It will be my pleasure to show you the stone books from which the recipe is drawn.'

'You have them here?' blurted Jed. 'In this building?'

'In this building, no. But *of* this building, yes.'

He reached to his side and took a long rolled piece of parchment and spread it across the table. It was a map of Prague. Andel pointed one bony finger, marking for them the building they sat in.

'Prague does not *contain* books of stone. It *is* a book of stone. Pictures and symbols hidden in plain sight for seekers to find.'

'You mean the signs on the houses?' asked Kassia.

The old man nodded. 'String together the images you need from the book of stone and you will find the recipe for the elixir you seek.'

Jed leant back in his chair. Is that what he as Fulcanelli had done? Connected together symbols and signs and found the recipe for everlasting life?

The old man glanced across the table at Jacob, who nodded for the man to go on.

'There's a test involved,' confirmed Andel. 'Each alchemist interprets the signs and symbols in his own way, and so it must be that a seeker finds six symbols from the stone book that mean the most to them. If you collect images of these six symbols and bring them to me by dawn tomorrow, and I verify the importance of the images you have chosen, then there's a chance that you'll be able to interpret your symbols to find the recipe.'

Jed looked across at Kassia. 'You want us to find symbols we *connect* to?'

The old man lowered his head a little. 'Yes. And if you choose well, then I will help you with the recipe.'

Jed's mind was whirring. How would they find the symbols they needed? If they had until dawn, then that was about eight hours. In the dark. Was the man playing with them? As if in answer to Jed's unspoken question, Andel stood up and walked over to a cabinet which ran along the far wall of the room. He took a small packet from the top. Then, with the other hand, he took three small glass bottles and carried them with him, putting them side by side on the nearest corner of the unrolled map. He opened the packet and slid out a deck of cards.

They were unlike normal playing cards. There was a picture on each one but it was hard for Jed to see them clearly as Andel shuffled the pile, then selected three, one by one, and placed them face up on the table.

The three cards were edged in different colours.

Across the centre of each was a drawing of a glass flask containing a golden liquid. Andel ordered the cards precisely and tapped them in turn: first the one with the black border, then the one with the white and finally the red.

'These represent the three main stages of alchemy,' he said softly, as if he was speaking just for himself and not for those who sat around the table desperate to hear. 'Nigredo: black; Albedo: white; and finally Rubedo: red. I like to think of them as the three stages of the human condition. As part of your test, you must collect droplets of these stages from the seeker in your team you believe is most connected to the images from the book of stone. Bring the droplets to me. These, combined with the images you choose, will form the basis of your recipe.'

'But I'm confused. What do we do when we've found all this stuff?' said Kassia.

'Meet me at the astronomical clock in the town square by six a.m.' He gestured down at the cards and empty glass vials. 'Take these with you. You will find torches in the hallway.'

Jed stood up. 'But I'm not sure we really understand. The vials? The symbols? Could you . . .'

Andel's rheumy eyes were suddenly steely blue again. 'It is a *test*, young sir,' he said quietly.

Jed felt his blood run cold.

Jacob stood up and made a grab for the bottles, cards and map. 'Until dawn, you say?'

Andel held Jed's gaze for just a second longer and then he nodded.

JUNE 29TH 1927

# DAY 60
## 28th April

'This makes no sense,' snapped Jed.

It was midnight. They were standing outside the House of the Stone Ram. The image carved between the windows no longer looked like a unicorn. More like a sheep waiting for slaughter.

It was cold and dark. And they had just six hours to complete a quest that not one of them really understood.

'What's with the bottles?' Kassia blurted.

'And how are we supposed to find the images we need?' Jed blew out a breath and covered his face with his hands. Suddenly, they were tugged free.

'What you doing, mate?' Dante's signs were huge.

Jed was taken aback. 'What?'

'Six hours to do this and you're feeling sorry for yourself?'

Sorry for himself. *Really?* He was just confused. 'But there're symbols everywhere,' he said defensively. 'We've seen them. On practically every building in Prague. How do we know which ones we need?'

'Welcome back to *my* world,' said Dante. He gestured with his hands pressing down towards his head. 'So much information. So many signs. And I have to filter it all.'

Jed looked at him as if seeing his silence for the first time.

'Every minute. Every day. I'm trying to work out what I should focus on,' explained Dante. 'And it's like everybody's hands are screaming as they wave them around. But not everyone's fingers are talking. It's a blur of movement noise and I have to shut out all the rubbish and focus in. And that's what you need to do now!'

'OK.' Jed didn't know what else to say.

'And it might have helped if you'd eaten more of your goulash,' Dante signed, almost apologetically.

'So we just wander around then, looking for signs and choose six, right?'

Kassia stepped in closer. 'I was thinking that if we're supposed to choose signs that you most *connect* to, then maybe you should try and see that dragon thing you talk about. It could help.'

'I don't want to see that!' Jed pressed his hands to his face again, as if this time he was more determined than ever to shut out everything around him. The visions had begun in London. Circling faces. Numbers. Dates. And they'd become stronger; the sensation of seeing them, more intense.

Kassia tugged his hands away this time. 'I don't think you have a choice.'

'But it feels like I'm drowning! I can only just about keep things together if I focus on the here and now!'

'You have to think about the past, Jed. How can you connect to the images in this great big stone book we're supposed to be reading, if you don't do that?'

Maybe he didn't want to connect. No good had come of any of the memories of the past. How could he really think about being an old man with a past, trapped inside the body of a young man without a future? How would that help? And how could he possibly tell the others about how terrified it made him to see even snatches of memories that might be his? He tried desperately to divert the conversation. 'What about the bottles?'

'No clue,' said Kassia. 'But it will come to us.'

'And if it doesn't?'

She unrolled the map in answer. Failing, it seemed, was apparently not up for discussion.

The map showed that Prague, like London and Heidelberg, was carved in half by the river. The Vltava separated the castle and Little Quarter from the Old and New Town and the Jewish Quarter. He stood up and looked to the left. According to the map, the astronomical clock was part of the Old Town Hall and not far away at all. So the end of the quest was easy to see. Less simple was finding the beginning. But some writing printed on the back of the map listed something called the Alchemical Path, so they agreed that using this as a framework might be a good idea.

They began to walk. The air was crisp. Street-lights bathed the cobbles in a pale and ghostly glow and in the half-light it was clearer to see how Prague was a place of two halves, not just of geography but of time as well. Centuries-old buildings down dusty alleys stood with stooped roofs and bowing windows, just as in wider streets modern neon signs flashed and flickered. Historic buildings housed travellers exhausted from their visits to art galleries and museums, as stag-night parties spilled out of bars, linking arms as they barrelled through the town in search of night-time entertainment. There was no traffic. Trams were empty and still at the side of the roads, as if abandoned. Sculptures and statues stared down from rooftops, gargoyles leered from guttering and at the corner of one narrow lane, a horse, free now of its carriage, stood waiting to be led away to its stable. Prague felt other-worldly: a mixture of centuries thrown into a pot and none of them fully dissolved, so that traces from one era bled into others. It felt as if the veil between what was and what could be was gossamer thin. Like the stars Jed had watched with Kassia in Heidelberg, past and present time fused together in a volatile mix of fire. It felt as if strange things could happen here.

So Jed did what he knew the others wanted him to, even though he was terrified. He tried to open himself up to memories. He looked for the spinning dragon round every corner.

The map showed them they'd reached something called the Powder Gate. It stood like a giant's wisdom tooth, roots drilling down to the ground, creating an arched space to walk under and through to the other side. Kassia angled her torch upwards, and sparks of gold flickered across the decorated stone.

'Angels,' said Jed, gesturing to the golden wings on the huge statues that stood as guards pressed into the stone. The Gate reached up into spires, each topped with steel spikes as if there to pierce the underside of drifting clouds and bring on the rain. On a single shaft, in front of the Gate, was a four-faced clock. Quarter past midnight. They had less than six hours.

'The path begins here,' said Jacob.

Jed searched for signs. Tried to plunge deep into his memory. Nothing.

Kassia steered him to the left. There was a squat building to the side of the Gate and its painted orange brickwork looked bright in the torchlight. Square, undecorated windows stared out into the street. Dante touched Jed's arms gently and pointed up.

Jed's stomach clenched. A sputtering of movement began inside his head. Not a spinning circle but an arc slicing into his vision like a knife scratching the final scrapings of butter across cold, burnt toast. Was this it? The first image? He tried to breathe. Go with the memory. But it hurt.

On the side of the building was a golden cage. Behind the grille was the statue of a mother and a child. They wore sparkling crowns above their black faces. The child held an orb in its hand like the one a king would carry.

'It's called a black Madonna,' said Kassia.

This meant nothing to Jed. The bars of the prison crisscrossed in his mind. He remembered the cage NOAH had forced him into in The Shard. The panic he'd felt then resurfaced like a fist breaking through water. But this wasn't one of the symbols they needed. This was linked to a new memory. One since the

Thames. And he knew he had to fight further back into his past. To memories still clothed in shadow.

They moved on.

Above them, statues leaned out from buildings and rooftops as if they wanted to whisper their secrets. In the darkness, gold images looked like flames, as if the rooftops and archways were flecked with fire. A golden angel inclined down towards them. He carried a laurel wreath in one hand and in the other a horn of fruit. Tucked beside the fruit was a long stick, and in the torchlight Jed could see a snake curled around it. Jed stared hard. The wreath reminded him of the sculpture of the cherubs back in Heidelberg, but it was not one of the six symbols they were supposed to collect either. This memory too was far too close. He had to go back further in his mind.

He was sure of this because of what happened when they turned the corner.

It felt as if the dragon image soared up from his stomach. It pushed behind his eyes and began to spin and spin, widening to engulf everything around him. It was dark, but light blazed behind his eyes. He felt so hot he could barely breathe. Sweat beaded on his forehead and he slumped to the ground as the light burst into blackness, thicker and heavier than the reality of the night.

'You see something?' blurted Kassia, kneeling beside him. 'Here? This house? There's a symbol here?'

Jed looked up and the dragon behind his eyes exploded and fell away. And above the doorway of the house in front of them, he saw the symbol of a blackened sun.

Jacob circled the location on the map. 'You're sure?' he said. 'That sun?'

Jed pressed his hand hard against the ground. 'I'm sure.'

'Why *that* symbol?' signed Dante.

Jed pretended he'd been unable to read Dante's signs.

'Jed! Why that one?' said Kassia leaning in.

'I don't know.' But he thought perhaps he did. It was just an inkling. An itch of a thought.

Kassia helped him to stand. 'Are you ready to move on?' she said, wiping her hands on her trousers.

Jed knew he mumbled his reply. He was embarrassed. About his sweaty palms. About the falling in the street. And unsure about how he could be so certain that the first image they needed was the one of a sun turned black.

The map told them they were moving south. They hurried together, none of them speaking as they stared up at building fronts, the arcs of their torchlights cutting the darkness. Kassia stopped every now and then and gestured questioningly. But there was nothing until they turned into a street called Rytirska.

The impact was sudden. Like a kick to the stomach. The dragon rose again, spinning so quickly this time that the world spun too and Jed staggered, steadying himself with his arms flung wide. They were in front of a house that was painted blue. At the top of the building there was a sculpture of a tomb. Angels were lifting the lid and skeletal faces peered out. Lower down on the wall of the house was another golden symbol. A wheel with eight spokes jutting from a central hub. In Jed's mind, the dragon became the wheel, turning and turning with such strength that it looked as if it would rip away from the wall of the house and career down the street. A train wheel, free of its fixing, spinning and spinning so that the train thundered from the track, throwing its carriages, spilling its goods and crashing. Jed heard screaming. Voices clamouring to be heard. Words he didn't recognise. But words he somehow understood. People were dying. Begging for their lives. And still the wheel spun on and on.

Jed's hands clutched at the wall but there was nothing to hold on to. He sank again to the curb and the concrete was cold against the back of his legs.

They needed the symbol of the golden wheel.

And this time he was certain he knew why.

'The dates,' he said quietly.

Kassia was kneeling. She reached forward as if perhaps she was going to hold on to his hands. But she hesitated.

'It's to do with the dates,' he said.

'You're not making sense, Jed.'

It made perfect sense to him. But how could he explain?

He looked across at Jacob. He'd been there. In the farmhouse in Spain. He would understand. And that night on the balcony with Kassia, looking at the stars. She would know if he could bear to string the ideas together for her.

'The perfect six,' he said.

Kassia wasn't following his logic. 'You have to tell me what you mean.'

'It's all connected. A giant wheel. And the wheel's important. It's the second memory. The second date.'

Dante was kneeling too now. Jed had no energy to sign but Dante wasn't angry. He was prepared to wait.

'When I first saw the dragon, there were numbers. And we worked out they were dates.'

'And that's how you knew,' said Kassia, 'that you'd taken the elixir five times and you needed to take it one more time.'

In the distance the screams came again and the golden wheel spun as if it was leaving tyre tracks in his heart. 'The first date was of a solar eclipse. It's why we need the blackened sun.'

'And the second date?' said Kassia gently.

'A train crash.' He could barely say the words. 'Hundreds died.'

'And you think those dates are when you took the elixir?' said Jacob, and Jed knew he was remembering the newspaper images they'd found back in the farmhouse.

Jed nodded.

'So all the symbols we need,' signed Dante slowly, 'will somehow connect to the five days from history.'

Again Jed nodded. 'And good things did not happen on those dates.' He was struggling to speak. 'We need images that connect to disasters.'

'So the third date?' asked Kassia gently.

It was Jacob who found the words Jed needed, obviously remembering the list he and Jed had made. 'The third date connects to poisoning. That's the next image we need.'

'And how long do we have left?'

'Four and a half hours,' said Jacob.

Dante helped Jed up as Jacob circled the second image on the map.

'Are you ready?' Kassia said gently.

'It doesn't matter if he's ready,' said Jacob. 'We have to press on.'

Jed saw a determination in Jacob's eyes that he hadn't seen before. The ground felt spongy under his feet and he leaned in heavily towards Dante's side.

They walked together, north this time, away from the house of the golden wheel.

They found somewhere called the Karolinum. A sprawling spread of buildings.

'This is part of the university, I think,' said Jacob, confirming this from the map.

Jed searched the stone for symbols. There was a shield built into the wall above two barred windows. A sculpted man kneeling in front of a sculpted king. They hurried on, past a wooden doorway cut into a bigger wooden door and capped with a balcony. Leaves and garlands made of stone crept down the pillars either side. But none of this was right. Finally, an oriel window that jutted out into the street. It looked like an enormous pulpit which had been dragged from a church and attached randomly to the side of the building. Tiny latticed panes of glass circled round the structure, bouncing back the light from their torches.

Jed needed to stop. Needed to breathe. He put out his hand to rest a moment against the cold dark stone.

A charge like electricity surged through his sweating fingers. He pulled back his hand and wobbled where he stood. Then the dragon spun again, closer and closer to his face until all he could see was a chink of light and a face. Not a living face. A face of stone at the top of one of the pillars supporting the window. It was circled, not only by the segmented body of the spinning dragon, but by leaves. And the leaves stretched from the man's face, his mouth wide, his eyes only slits and his features screwed up in pain, as the branches and foliage spilled from his jaw.

'There,' gasped Jed. 'The third image.'

Dante and Kassia helped him to sit.

He was sure he was going to be sick. Like the poisoned man above him. His forehead was slick with sweat. He could feel it soaking into his eyelashes.

'This is too much for him,' groaned Kassia. 'Every new image is worse. He can't keep doing this.'

She untucked her shirt from her jeans and used the edge of her top to wipe his face. And then she hesitated, her fingers clenched around the fabric, an idea forming in her mind. 'Do you trust me?' she said softly.

More than anyone. But he couldn't move his mouth to answer.

Kassia reached up to Jacob. 'A bottle. Pass me a bottle.'

Jacob fumbled in his pocket.

'Quickly.'

The dragon thrashed the air before Jed's eyes and he was sure he was going to pass out, but Kassia wiped his brow again and then unscrewed the bottle and squeezed the edge of her shirt over the opening. A single droplet of sweat ran from the fabric, snaking a line against the cold glass.

Jed gripped tight to the edge of the curb, begging silently for an explanation.

'Andel asked for droplets from the three stages of the human condition,' Kassia said quietly. 'I think sweat's one of them.'

Jed lowered his head. He was embarrassed. So awkward he couldn't look at her. The image of the three cards Andel had given them flickered in his memory. Nigredo, Albedo, Rubedo. Was sweat really one of the liquids they needed?

They waited for a moment. Jed's heartbeat was irregular, lurching and stumbling as if his heart had forgotten how to work properly. But the ticking of time remained unchanged.

'Less than four hours,' said Jacob. 'We have to keep moving.'

But Jed wasn't sure that he could.

\* \* \*

'He's burning up,' signed Dante.

Kassia looked at Jed's hunched body leaning forward over the gutter. His face was clammy and grey in the fragile light spilling from the street lamp, and his hands were trembling. He looked older than she'd ever seen him.

Dante hurried into the open-all-night pharmacy over the road and returned with a bottle of water. He knelt and pressed the bottle to Jed's lips. Jed drank, but water spilled and puddled on to the road.

Kassia grabbed her brother's arm and pulled him towards her. 'We have to stop this,' she said. 'It's too many memories, too soon. Look what they're doing to him.'

'We're halfway there,' said Dante. 'Just three more to go.'

'He can't cope,' Kassia insisted. 'Each memory's worse. And if they're connected to the dates, then they're getting closer to the here and now. The pain's just going to get worse.'

'So what's your solution? Do we give up?'

'No.'

'So what then? We're against the clock, Kass. And by my reckoning we have less than three hours.'

Kassia's own hands were starting to tremble.

Dante pulled her further down the street and

pointed upwards. He took her torch and threw the beam of light against the brickwork. An iron rod stuck out of the wall. Hanging from it was a chain. On the chain, a clump of what looked like blackened cloth was suspended. Dante put the end of the torch in his mouth so the beam of light held steady on the wall, leaving his hands free to speak. 'Do you know what that is?' he signed.

Kassia had no clue.

'It's a human hand,' signed Dante. 'A thief's hand, cut off years ago and hung there as a warning.'

'That's gross!'

'Yep. But like all the symbols in this weird city, it's there to mean something.'

'Hanging a human hand up means something?' said Kassia incredulously.

Dante turned her round to face him. The torch shone in her eyes making her blink. 'We have to keep doing this, Kass. Because if we don't, something will steal Jed from us.'

Kassia didn't want her brother to go on. She knew he was talking about death. A thief who came in the night. 'OK. I get it. But I'm scared.'

Dante pulled her into a hug. It was his way of saying he knew. When he spoke with words again his hands moved more gently. 'What's the thing with the bottles?'

'I think I know what three liquids we need.'

'The first being sweat?' signed Dante.

Kassia ran her finger round the top of the bottle in her pocket.

'And the other two?'

'Will be harder to collect,' she said.

Back at the side of the street, Jacob was helping Jed to stand. 'Fourth date,' said Jacob. 'A hurricane. More tricky this one, but the symbol has to stand for wind, which we can't see.'

'That's the point of symbols,' agreed Dante. 'So we need an image that stands for something else. The power of nature, that kind of thing.'

Kassia moved to the other side of Jed. 'You sure you want to keep going?' she said quietly. 'Dante says we mustn't stop but you look terrible and I'm worried.'

'Dante's right,' he whispered. 'Not about everything.' There was an attempt at a smile. 'But he's right about this. And about the symbols I think.'

Kassia's hand brushed against his. It was still wet with sweat. She pulled her hand away awkwardly.

They walked slowly. Kassia could hear Jed's breathing rattling in his chest. 'Where does it hurt?' she said.

This time the smile reached his eyes. 'Everywhere.'

He shuffled forwards. 'It's like I see the events as if I'm there. And I suppose, I was.'

Kassia didn't know how to respond.

Dante shone the torch up at buildings as they passed, flashing light on to darkness. A new stone face stared down at them from his fixed position above a doorway. At first glance, the face looked human, until the arc of the torchlight caught the points of horns on his head. Then, as the light stretched, Kassia saw great bat wings straining behind the seated stone figure. 'It's the devil,' she whispered quietly. And the devil held the world in his hand as they walked on.

Jed's step was slowing. Kassia's heart was quickening. And a breeze was blowing in from the river.

Suddenly, Jed grabbed at his head and lurched towards the wall. Dante reached out and helped steer him to the ground.

'Here, Jed?' Kassia said urgently. 'Is the symbol here?'

When Jed looked at her, his skin was the colour of wet clay that had been left too long in the sun. Lines cracked beside his eyes as if the effort of searching was literally breaking him. Kassia scoured the building beside them for clues. What symbol had he seen? What image did they need?

The wooden doorway was surrounded by extravagant stone pillars carved to look like branches.

A stone frieze ran across the top of the door frame. At either side, standing proud of the stone, was a sculpted bear. Each beast looked forward, head bowed, front paw lifted. The bears were ready to fight. Was this the symbol? The strength of nature ready to take on humans?

'Are you sure, Jed? This is for the hurricane?'

'Look,' he said, raising his shaking hand and pointing. 'I think those men are trying to control the bears, but they can't.'

Kassia saw two sculpted men kneeling in front of the stone animals. She could tell they were powerless.

Jed was looking down again. And suddenly, Kassia's fear was overtaken by her determination to make things OK. 'You do believe nature can be beaten, don't you?' she pleaded. 'Listen to me, Jed. This search for symbols is just what it is. It's not a sign about what's *going* to happen. Just what *did*.'

He didn't look like he believed her.

She grabbed Jacob's arm. 'Another bottle. I need another bottle.'

Jacob scrabbled in his pocket and passed one over.

She'd wanted to wait. Make sure Jed could cope with all six images, but now that seemed like a dangerous strategy. He was losing strength all the time.

She knelt in front of Jed and stared hard into his

face. 'I think I know about the three liquids and what we need to collect next.'

His eyes were glassy and she wasn't sure that he could focus on her.

'Do you have the watch I gave you?'

Jed looked confused, but he reached into his pocket and took out the silver pocketwatch that had been her father's. The casing was scratched from their time in the River Neckar, but she could still see the single swallow engraved on the back.

She opened the casing. Her heart stumbled as she registered the time. Just over two hours. That's all they had left.

She bit her lip to stop it shaking and twisted the top of the watch face. The silver casing turned and loosened and the glass disc that protected the face rattled loose. Kassia pulled the encasement away and took the disc in her hand. She wiped it and the misting caused by the river water disappeared. But she hadn't removed the glass for cleaning. She'd taken it out of the watch to use it.

The edge of the disc was exactly as she hoped. Razor sharp.

'You said you trusted me. I think the second liquid needed is your blood.'

Jed looked at her in horror.

'Sweat. And blood,' said Kassia, offering Jed the disc. 'Do you think you can?'

Jed waited for a second as the uncovered hands of the watch ticked onwards, unchecked.

Then he took the glass disc and he closed his fingers around it, gripped tight into a fist.

And as the watch ticked onwards, a single rivulet of blood snaked towards his wrist.

Kassia fumbled with the bottle, undid the lid and then held it against his skin. And the blood splashed into the container.

When the drops of blood had covered the base, Kassia pulled it away and fastened the lid. Then she prized Jed's fingers open. The watch face was edged with blood, the cut in his hand like a vivid lifeline across his palm.

Kassia took the disc and wiped it clean on her shirt. Then she put it back on the watch and tightened the casing. The watch ticked on but now the face was misted with blood, not water from a river. She slipped the bottle into her pocket. It clinked against the other one. Sweat. And blood.

You know what the fifth date is, don't you?' said Jacob.

Kassia felt as if her stomach had turned to water. It was the date her father had died.

Jed had seen the date carved on her dad's gravestone back in London. He'd realised then that it was important and so when memories of numbers had started to return, it had gradually become clear that these were dates too. Of the days he'd taken the elixir. It meant that when her father had been dying, Jed had been fighting death as well. Her father had lost. And Jed had won.

So what did they need as a record of that day? A symbol of death built into the book of stone. But nearly all the dates they'd collected already had included death. The train wreck; the hurricane; the poisoning. Hundreds had died. Didn't all the symbols they'd chosen represent death in some way, if you looked close enough to see what the images really said?

Yes. But in order to complete the task, they needed a symbol of something else that had happened on that day. But how could anything else matter in the hours in which her father had been taken from her? How could anything be important, compared to that? Kassia wiped her face and began to walk.

'I don't think I can do this,' Kassia said. Her mouth was silent. Only her fingers spoke. Her words were only for her brother.

'We have to,' Dante signed. 'This is about more than Dad.'

'How can you say that?' her signs were as sharp as the circle of glass that had cut into Jed's hand.

Dante looked angry. 'Don't make this about who loved Dad more, Kass. You have no idea how hard it is for me now that he's gone.'

Kassia flung her hands up to protest. Tears burned behind her eyes. But Dante grabbed her arms and pushed them to her side. 'This is about what else happened that day. Understand!'

He began to walk and Jacob followed: Jed leaning against him, limping now. Jed's hand hung loose by his side and, in the flickering light of the street lamp, Kassia could still see the bracelet of dried blood that wove round his wrist.

They walked through the cobbled lanes and alleys and the air was crisp. The first tiny traces of sunlight were bleeding into the edge of the sky. It was nearly morning.

The light from the torches seemed feeble suddenly against the gathering dawn. Fighting earlier with the darkness of night, the light had seemed strong, but now the beams were weak and ineffectual. Kassia looked up as gargoyles leered from gutters. A sculpted man sat astride a sculpted lion in frozen prowl on a rooftop. Spires jabbed at the sky.

And it was as the darkness turned to the soft shades

of a ripening peach, and all these images became clearer, that Jacob called to them that they only had an hour and a half left. Then Jed stopped walking.

They'd climbed north, away from the Old Town Square and up towards the highest curve of the river. On the building in front of them, inside a huge triangle of stone sitting proud above a doorway, was a sign that had been painted. A human face inside a blazing, golden sun.

Kassia remembered. The heatwave in France. The reason the police thought her father might have been distracted as he drove. The reason for the crash. The sun. The fifth symbol.

Jacob circled the location on the map.

They had five of the six images. They'd filled two of the three bottles.

One image and one bottle left.

Kassia thought about her dad. She thought of how he'd made her mum learn sign language to speak to Dante when everyone else had thought he should learn to speak with his voice. Her father had always done the unexpected. Broken the rules her mum loved so much.

Her dad would understand what she was going to do now, even if nobody else did.

* * *

ALBEDO

RUBEDO

028
022

20km
48° 52' 54"
2° 41' 47"
48.88167°
2.69639°

510. LOCOMOTIVES DE FR

Locomotive compound à surchauffe, 4 cylindres, n° 24
construite par les anciens Établisseme

057206-2W
2775

- (Est. série 13, nᵒˢ 241.001 à 241.041)

EST 241040

ype Mountain, pour trains rapides très lourds,
il et Cⁱᵉ, à Denain, en 1932.

December 23rd

Jed wiped the dried blood from his wrist. His palm stung; the cut throbbing as he gingerly moved his fingers.

He hadn't realised it would be so difficult. Collect images, Andel had said. Connect to the symbols of the city. He'd no idea that doing this would open the wounds of the past, just like he'd willingly opened the gash on his own hand. He'd spent the last few months trying to remember. And then trying to forget. And now his mind felt like a sponge that had taken on too much water. Memories were leaking all around him.

There'd been voices, all of them begging for help. And so much pain. Not just his own, but from people he saw in his mind, like blurred photographs. He'd been at all those places; when the sun had darkened and then when it had shone so brightly people had died in the heat. And it was as if each memory was a punishment for taking the elixir.

Five times he'd drunk the medicine to bring about eternal life. Were the pain and the elixir connected? Had what he'd done caused the disasters he remembered? Was this the result of playing God? He didn't know.

And he also didn't know where the next image would come from. Five dates. Five images. But Andel had asked for six.

'I think we should go to the river.' Kassia had sat down beside him on the curb.

'I'm not sure.' He was scared of moving anywhere.

'You've used up all the days you took the elixir, but the river is always important. The Thames. The Neckar. The Vltava must be too.'

Jed had no energy to find words to answer her.

'And I think we should go alone,' she said.

He certainly had no energy to argue.

'Dante and Jacob are going to meet us at the astronomical clock,' she said. 'We have an hour.'

It didn't seem possible that the night was nearly over. The cobbles had begun to glint in the first strains of sunshine. The street lamps were switched off, torches no longer needed. Kassia waited as Jed pushed himself to standing. And then they began to walk, south this time, through the city as it began to wake.

The Charles Bridge, which spanned the Vltava, was as wide as a four-lane road. Gothic towers, with turrets and rooftop spikes, guarded each section where the bridge connected to the land and along the side of the structure, rising up from the sandstone walls, were at least thirty huge stone statues, equally spaced, like a welcoming guard. Sculpted priests and rulers, saints and saviours looked inwards to the centre of the bridge, watching over travellers who wanted to walk from one side to the other.

Jed did not want to cross the bridge.

His mind flashed back to the Thames and how he'd fought to keep alive. And then to the Neckar and how he'd been sure that Kassia had drowned.

'Please,' he said quietly. 'I can't do this.'

Kassia turned towards him and even in the half-light of the morning he could see that something had changed. Her face looked hardened, like the chiselled stone of the faces all around him. 'Don't you think I'm scared of the river too?'

'Of course you're scared. I'm sorry, it's just . . .'

He wobbled a little but she didn't move forward to support him. 'You think this is all about you. Have you got any idea what I've given up to be here?'

'Of course I have.'

'Really?' She spat the word. 'My mum had all these plans for me and I've risked all of that for you and now when we're so close to the answers, you're scared to cross the river?'

Where was this coming from? He'd never seen her so angry.

'You can't possibly know how it feels to disappoint her. You have no family!'

He felt her words like a punch to the stomach.

More painful than any of the memories sparked by words in the stone book they'd been reading. These words were sharp and real.

'Kassia, please. I don't understand—'

She gave him no time to finish. She was pacing, her trainers scuffing hard against the cobbles. 'You don't understand! What about me? My life in London torn apart by you and what you've done.'

Her face was far from stone now. It was very much alive.

He reached towards her in desperation. 'Please.'

'Don't touch me!' she yelled. 'I don't want you to come anywhere near me. You've ruined everything!'

The world around him tilted as if he was on a boat and things were sliding off the deck into the sea. He slumped down to the ground. Everything they'd been through in the river and in the hospital meant nothing then. What he'd done. Who he was. It repulsed her.

She was standing by a sculpture of a man whose head was ringed with golden stars. 'See this guy,' she said, waving wildly at the information plate beside the statue. 'Crowds turned against him and threw him into the river.'

Jed couldn't look. He wanted to press his hands to his ears and drown out her rage.

'They should have done that to you! You've played around with life and death and that's what you deserve!'

So that's what she wanted. Him dead. Not the elixir at all. He could hardly breathe and suddenly he understood that perhaps it would be better if there really was no more air in his lungs. Maybe it would be better if it ended here. Beside a different river.

Pain like fire burned behind his eyes and he lowered his head into his hands.

Suddenly, Kassia was kneeling beside him.

She fumbled in her pocket then swept his flopping fringe away from his eyes. With a shaking hand she held the final glass bottle to his cheek. A single tear splashed into the glass. 'I'm so sorry,' she mumbled. 'I didn't mean it. I promise I didn't mean it. It's just . . .'

His stomach folded. Words bounced on his tongue, fighting to be the first spoken. 'What?'

'I'm so sorry!' She was fumbling with the bottle, tightening the lid to keep the tears inside.

'What are you doing?' He tried to pull himself away. She'd gone totally mad. One minute she was shouting and wanting him dead and the next she was kneeling beside him begging him to forgive her.

'Jed, please. Let me explain.' Kassia was tugging his

arms to make him look at her. 'Tears,' she said quietly. 'We needed your blood, your sweat and your tears.' She was sobbing now. 'It was the only way.'

He pulled back from her. 'A trick? To make me cry?'

'I'm so sorry,' she said again. 'How else could I have done it?'

'You didn't mean what you said? It was all some sort of trick?'

Her horror was real. Not a mask. Suddenly the pain in his palm didn't matter.

'You don't hate me?'

'No!' She held the glass bottle up and the tears trapped inside sparkled in the strengthening sun of the morning.

'What if it hadn't worked? That was a dangerous game you were playing!'

Her cheeks flushed red. 'I'm getting quite used to danger,' she said.

He tried to smile. He could see that she was shaking.

For the first time since stepping on to the bridge, Jed looked down towards the water. 'Promise me that in future the river will be a place we come to when things are going well,' he said gently. 'I'd kind of like some good memories to be connected to rivers.'

She smiled. 'OK, River Boy. New plan. We'll make rivers good places. Bridges too, if you like.'

'I'd like that,' sighed Jed. 'Places we could go and just be OK.'

They sat for a moment watching the water flow beneath them. The gap between them was as thin as paper. Kassia could almost feel the rise and fall of Jed's shoulders. She wanted that moment to stretch on unbroken.

'How long have we got?' Jed asked eventually.

'Twenty minutes.'

'And the last image? You think it's from one of these statues on the bridge?'

She looked along the line of stone figures. 'It can't be a memory of a day you took the elixir, so it has to be something new.'

Jed took a deep breath and stood up tentatively as if unsure he had the strength to hold his own weight. 'What about the guy who was thrown in the river?' he said.

They faced the statue and Jed ran his hand across a metal frieze that explained the history. It showed John Nepomuk being tossed by a crowd from the side of the bridge. The image of his body shone more brightly than the rest of the metal plaque. It had been polished clean by fingers over time. 'People touch this image for luck,' Jed said.

'So you think this is the final image we need?'

Jed pressed his own finger against the metal. He expected it to be cold, but it felt as if there was heat trapped inside. 'Did he die?' he scanned the writing for more information.

Kassia nodded. 'But look at his statue.'

Jed looked up at the sculpted man. The halo of stars shone around his head.

'People realised they'd made a mistake,' she said. 'He was a good man. People understood that in the end.'

Jed held out his hand for the map and pen and Kassia passed it to him. The three glass bottles clinked against each other in her pocket as she moved. Jed circled the final location on the map. Blood, sweat and tears. And the final image found. It was time to meet Andel and the others at the clock. They'd finally read the story of the stone book of Prague. Now they needed his help to work out what it meant. And they had less than twenty minutes to get there.

The bottles bounced in Kassia's pocket as they hurried towards the Old Town Square and the meeting place by the astronomical clock. Jed didn't have the energy to run yet, but his strength was returning; the pain in his head dulling a little. Strangely, being by the river had made him feel stronger. Perhaps it was from the relief of knowing that Kassia hadn't meant all the horrible things she'd said.

There was a gaggle of people already at the foot of the clock tower when they burst into the Old Town Square. 'What's going on?' Jed demanded.

'Just tourists,' Kassia reassured. 'They're waiting for the clock to strike. Come on. It's nearly six.'

'But the thing just tells the time, right?'

'More than that, I think.' She pointed up at the two huge circular faces on the side of the Old Town Hall. Dials turned within dials; blue, gold and yellow in the growing light of morning. 'I guess that's some sort of calendar too.' She pointed up to the highest dial. 'And that can't just be the time here, can it? Looks like it has the time of other places too.'

The crowd pressed forward. 'Weird,' Jed said, almost to himself. 'How we make up time and it can be different in different places.' His head began to throb again, as if the energy required to think about this was as much as he'd have needed to run.

'So where's Andel?' urged Kassia, scanning the crowd and pulling him forward. 'We have to find him before six.'

Jed pointed to the left. He could just make out Dante and Jacob standing to the side of the clock. The old man from the House of the Stone Ram was

126

standing between them. According to the watch in his pocket they still had five minutes, but the way the crowd pressed forward in expectation of the clock's striking made him doubt they'd be in time.

Dante saw them first and held his hand up and waved them over. Jed stumbled to a standstill.

'You have all six images?' asked Andel.

'Yes.' Jed couldn't help but pant. 'And the bottles.'

'Good.'

Jed stared at the old man. *Good?* That was all he was going to say? They'd been racing around the city for six hours, dragging through memories that tore his insides apart and the old man just said 'good'! Jed glanced at Jacob. Seriously? What were they waiting for exactly? They'd read the stone book. Now they needed the recipe.

As if sensing Jed's discomfort, the old man smiled. 'I know you want answers. But there's no need to rush the final stages. As a guest in our great city, I insist you watch our wonderful clock in action.'

Jed opened his mouth to argue, but Dante trod down hard on his foot. Jed grimaced. There'd been no sign language but Jed supposed it was Dante's way of urging patience. But Jed didn't want to watch some stupid clock striking the hour while tourists took selfies. He wanted answers.

FOR P = 2: $2^1(2^2 - 1) = 6$
FOR P = 3: $2^2(2^3 - 1) = 28$
FOR P = 5: $2^4(2^5 - 1) = 496$
FOR P = 7: $2^6(2^7 - 1) = 8128$

Jed was sure he saw a tiny glimmer behind the old man's eyes. He was going to enjoy stringing things out. 'You know alchemists of old kept their elixirs inside clocks,' Andel said. 'It made the power of the remedy more potent and more long-lasting.'

Jed didn't want to know about where elixirs were stored in the past. He wanted to know about how to make one now. He rummaged in his pocket for the map with the circled locations but Andel turned his head away and looked at the clock. 'All in good time. You need to see this.'

Suddenly, the crowd hushed. At the top of the clock tower, a mechanical figure of a skeleton pulled on a rope with his bony right hand. In the other hand he held an hourglass which he raised and then inverted.

'Death,' whispered Andel.

To the side of the mechanical skeleton, and above the highest clock face, two small doorways opened, revealing arches and a line of waiting statues. As the clock struck the hour, the statues began to move forward and process on a hidden track above the face of the clock.

'Are those the apostles?' asked Kassia, watching intently.

'How on earth d'you know that?' signed Dante.

'There're twelve of them. And they have halos, so I'm just guessing.'

'You're right, young lady. Apostles yes,' said Andel. 'But you might like to know that Judas has been replaced by St Paul. There is no place for Judas the betrayer with the twelve.'

Jacob lurched a little to the side. Jed moved to steady him. Jacob pulled his arm away and the base of a tattoo rippled on the muscles of his arm, beneath the turn of his sleeve. He'd obviously removed the bandage.

Jed remembered it had been hours since Jacob had eaten. He'd missed the goulash when the others had stopped for food, because he'd been trying to convince Andel to talk to them. He was obviously weak. Now the old man was insisting they watched some tourist attraction instead of doing what he'd promised.

'Please, sir,' Jed could wait no longer. 'We've done what you asked and you promised you'd help us understand the recipe.'

Andel kept his face on the clock as the final figures moved behind the open doors which closed behind them. On the top of the clock tower a real life trumpeter began to play. Andel allowed the notes to finish before he finally turned to face them. 'I will assess your completion of the test. And if I am satisfied,

I will help you with the recipe. But not here.'

Jed couldn't believe what he was hearing. What did he mean, not here?

'We can't work amongst these crowds.'

Jed bunched his hand into a fist and made to step forward, but Dante trod down once again on his foot. 'Keep it calm, mate,' Dante signed in miniature, his hands out of Andel's eyeline. 'Don't upset him.'

Jed pulled his foot away, but this time Jacob made a grab for him. 'Whoah, steady there. You're still shattered from the symbol hunt.'

They were making it sound like a game. And Jed wanted answers. He pulled himself away from Jacob's hold but Kassia stepped in front of him. 'It's OK,' she whispered and her words were warm against his skin.

His eyes locked on hers. It's OK, she said again, but she used no words.

Jed swallowed hard, flexing his fingers to release the tension in his hand. Then he nodded slowly.

'And we can't go back to the house of testing,' added Andel. 'There's something I need you to see.'

'So where are you taking us?' asked Jed, choking back the urge to shout the question.

'We need to look out over the top of the stone book you've been reading.' The old man shuffled forward a little, making his way out of the crowd. 'Seeing Prague from a great height will make everything clear. And so you need to come with me to the Petřín Tower.'

Jed followed the old man as he led them onwards. Behind them, the clock finished its impressive display. A mechanical cockerel crowed three times and the crowd began to thin. The show was over.

Andel explained the history as they walked. The Petřín Tower was on the top of a huge hill. The metal structure looked like a mini replica of the Eiffel Tower in Paris and was over one hundred years old. Flower gardens surrounded it and these had been developed to disguise the huge gashes in the ground caused when the workers of Prague had collected stone to build their city. The stone book, it seemed, began its writing in the gardens of Petřín. Kassia presumed that this was the reason Andel insisted they should go there.

It was possible to walk to the summit but the ground on the hill was so overgrown and dangerous underfoot that the safest and easiest way was to take the train.

Kassia had been on a funicular railway before. In Heidelberg. Two cables ran from the top of the hill to the station at the bottom. One carriage was attached to each cable and as one ascended the incline, another climbed down. The two vehicles worked in counterbalance to each other.

The station at the base of the hill was a small green, brick building. The door was locked and a notice in Czech seemed to suggest that the railway didn't start running until 9 a.m. Andel was undaunted by this. He took three keys from his pocket, selected one, then opened the station door, closing and locking it again once everyone was inside. The space was eerily quiet. In Heidelberg, the carriage up to the castle had been full of eager tourists but the lack of visitors here made the air reverberate strangely, their footsteps and voices echoing in the space that was closed in by high brick walls.

'Climb aboard,' said Andel, opening the door to the waiting carriage. 'Secrets await you.' He took a second key and fiddled with the dashboard. As the train began to move, a beacon light began to spin on the station wall, filling the train with an unnatural orange glow.

Kassia looked across at Jed. He seemed to be growing more agitated with every minute and she noticed that his hand was trembling. Collecting images from around the city had obviously exhausted him. She could only hope the ride to the summit was quick and that Andel's explanation of the recipe was just as speedy.

The carriage pulled out of the station and began to climb. Kassia leant back against the metal support that acted as a seat as the carriage pulled out of the brick-built pit and open land spread out on either side of the track. The air rushed past as the wheels clicked over the rails. Kassia focused on the cable. She didn't like to think about what would happen if it snapped.

Midway up the hill, the track began to bulge to the side. The single track was splitting in two and as they moved closer to the bulge, Kassia saw the second carriage appearing over the crest of the hill and gliding towards them. It was completely empty and moved silently past them like a ghost carriage. Kassia resisted the urge to stretch her hand to the window. The empty carriage looked close enough to touch.

The wheels clicked over a join in the track and then veered to the right, the double track restricting again to become one rail. To the side there was a stopping place. Kassia guessed if the train had been running to a normal timetable it might have paused here. It didn't. Andel was at the front of the train. He pressed buttons on the console and the carriage moved onwards, under a narrow bridge, and smoothly up the hill.

The journey to the Tower took about nine minutes.

Kassia stepped out of the carriage and Andel glanced over his shoulder to check that they followed. She'd expected the gardens to be full of tourists like the Old Town Square had been, but without the train running to bring people to the top of the hill, the place was deserted. A man was hunched over a spade, digging in a flower bed. He was dressed in a sleeveless green boiler suit and he kept his face firmly turned from the visitors as they emerged from the train. He drove the blade of the spade deep into the soil, his rhythm stumbling only slightly as an acknowledgement of their arrival.

Andel ignored the gardener.

'We're really close,' whispered Kassia, falling into step beside Jed. 'He's got to tell us everything, when we hand over the stuff we've found.'

Jed's agitation was sparking in his eyes. 'Something doesn't feel right.'

Kassia looked down at his hand. It was still shaking.

'Not with me,' Jed said defensively. 'I mean yep, I feel all wrong. But that's to do with the memories. Something feels wrong about *this*.'

'He wanted us to be alone,' encouraged Kassia.

'Well he certainly got his wish. Where is everyone?'

'Still down in the square waiting for that clock to chime again, I guess.'

Jed didn't look convinced by her suggestion.

'And what's with this tower? Do you think he

knows? About me? About how I'm from Paris, I mean?'

Kassia couldn't see how the old man could have worked anything out. They'd been careful and done just what he'd asked them and nothing more. How could the old guy possibly know Jed was Fulcanelli?

She'd had no time to even answer her own question before they'd reached the entrance to the huge metal tower which stretched out of a squat, hexagonal, wooden building. The door was locked. Andel used the third key. The old man squinted dismissively in the direction of the gardener and led the group inside.

'Let's take the elevator,' he said.

Kassia was incredibly grateful. The tower was made of a network of interlaced metal which crisscrossed its way up into the sky. Stairs corkscrewed upwards inside and she could tell there must be hundreds of them. They'd been up all night and she was exhausted. Not climbing stairs seemed like a perfect idea.

The elevator was tiny. Andel shut the door as they tumbled inside. Kassia watched as he then tugged down on a sheet of metal hanging from the ceiling at the edge of the elevator. This metal was a second door. As it slid down and locked into place, Andel mumbled about the brilliance of the extra security provided by this metal hatch door. He turned to the control panel. There was a basic picture of the tower's shape on the panel showing that there was a viewing platform half way up. Andel ignored the button for the midway platform and pressed the button to send them to the top. As the elevator climbed silently, small red electric lights lit up on the picture of the tower to show their position. The elevator juddered a little as the final light lit up. Andel pushed the metal door upwards and it ran into the roof space. Then he opened the second door and led out on to the top viewing platform.

Just for a moment, Kassia forgot why they'd come. Prague spread out around the tower, terracotta rooftops bright in the light of morning. The Vltava sparkled like a wet ribbon, and the green of the parkland looked like a blanket. Kassia stepped over to the handrail. At any other time she might have thought the view beautiful, but the realisation that they'd come here for information hit her like the cold of the air.

'So what did you want to show us up here?' Jed said.

Andel had moved away from the edge of the viewing platform and was standing in front of a set of metal binoculars angled out towards the view. 'Not so fast. You have the results of your test to show me.'

Dante looked across at Kassia for translation and she fumbled the old man's request into signs as Jed took the map from his pocket. Jacob looked on nervously. He'd said hardly anything on the journey. Even in the elevator, he'd been quiet.

Andel took the map Jed offered. 'So talk me through the symbols you chose.'

Kassia wasn't sure Jed would be able to. 'Do you want me to?' she asked.

'No. It's OK.' Jed's answer didn't sound that certain but she waited for him to carry on anyway.

He took each of the symbols in turn, pointing at their location on the map as he explained.

After the fifth symbol, he glanced across at her and she nodded to reassure him. 'And the final symbol we chose is of a man being thrown into a river,' he said, and as his hand pointed at this location on the map, his finger quivered.

There was creaking from the tower.

Kassia wasn't sure how she'd expected the old man to react to the images they'd collected. But she had expected *something*. Instead Andel looked across at Jacob. 'And the bottles of liquid I asked you to collect?'

Kassia fumbled in her pocket. She took first the sweat and the tears and then, when the old man had tucked these into his own pocket, she took the bottle of blood and held it out.

And then in that moment, several seemingly unconnected things happened all at once.

The creaking from the tower stopped. A door slammed shut. They were no longer alone on the viewing platform.

Andel looked to the side. He smiled at the newcomer and spoke quickly. 'I've delayed them just as you wished.'

The hand of a man in a green boiler suit grabbed for the bottle of blood.

Eyes sharp blue. Hair blond, slicked tight to his skull.

And Kassia realised, he was not a gardener.

Jed had no idea how NOAH had found them.

Cole stuffed the bottle of blood inside the boiler suit he'd worn as disguise. Then he lurched forward, flinging his arms wide.

Jed had seconds to react and he moved on instinct. He backed against the railings of the viewing platform, the metal binoculars on their rigid stand, a barrier between him and the man who was trying to capture him. The binoculars were on a pivot. You could pull them back to make it possible for shorter people to see through the lenses and angle the device precisely at the view. Jed drove his hand down on the metal support and then shoved the binoculars sharply to the left. They thumped into Cole's gut as he darted forward.

Cole clutched his stomach and staggered, winded from the impact. His bicep muscles spasmed. The tattoo of a unicorn in chains, straining up towards his shoulder, flexed and faltered. It gave Jed just the time he needed.

He grabbed Kassia's hand and charged towards the elevator. Jacob and Dante thundered behind them as Cole struggled to regain his breath. They reached the elevator and flung themselves inside. Jed strained upwards to grab the hatch door. But someone else was racing across the viewing platform towards them. Victor, dressed in green too. Cole had not been alone. This was an ambush.

Jed grabbed the underneath of the hatch door, but Victor lurched forward violently, reaching for Jed's arm. A pain seared through Jed's elbow but he scrabbled again for the underside of the rolling door as Dante shoulder-barged Victor away from the elevator opening. But Dante's forward momentum carried him back outside on to the viewing platform.

Kassia grabbed for her brother's jacket and tugged him back into the elevator just as Jed freed the rolling hatch door above them and hauled it down. He jabbed at the buttons on the wall. The elevator began to descend.

Everyone spoke at once; voices and hands mixing the words into a maelstrom. How had NOAH found them? How had the old man betrayed them? How could things have turned so quickly from being on the verge of getting the recipe, to this?

Jed held his hands up for calm. They were OK. They needed to focus on that. The elevator was halfway to the ground and there was no way Cole and Victor would get to the bottom of the stairs before them. They'd got away.

Then the elevator juddered to a halt.

Jed thumped the buttons on the wall. 'Come on! Come on!' Nothing.

All the lights in the lift marking their descent blazed red.

Dante thumped the buttons too. Still no change.

Jed looked at the door.

The plan was unspoken but it was clear there was no other way. The rolled hatch door ensured the elevator car was still sealed. Jed bent down and scrabbled at the base, pressing his fingers in the gap where the door connected to the floor. He strained upwards. The rolling door began to rise.

Dante worked with him until they'd pushed the door clear and it had rolled out of sight past the top of the metal box they were travelling in. But the elevator was out of position. It wasn't scheduled to stop at this location on the tower and there was nowhere for the rolling door to slide to: no magnetic fixers to latch it in place as there were at the very top or the very bottom of the shaft.

Through the newly formed opening, Jed could see the crisscrossed network of the metal tower. There was a gap between the shaft and the stairs which twisted like the ones in a helter-skelter all around the edge of the structure. Jed's arms were shaking under the weight of the door but he and Dante couldn't let go. If they did, it would just crash back into place and trap them again, inside the stationary elevator.

'OK,' said Jed, scrabbling to formulate a plan. 'Kassia, you and Jacob climb out. Get on the stairs. Then us.'

'One of you can't hold the weight of that!' said Kassia.

'I'll have to!'

'Maybe we should just stay here,' suggested Jacob. 'Hope the guys from NOAH run to the bottom and think we've left.'

Jed couldn't believe what he was hearing. 'They've stopped the elevator! Of course they'll know we're here!'

'OK.' Jacob moved forward towards the opening. 'I'll go first so I can help you out.'

There was a cavity of about a metre between the

elevator and the edge of the stairs. Metal bars latticed the sides so Jacob needed to stretch across the gap and climb through the interlaced metal. Jed tried not to think about how high up they were. He tried not to let his mind go anywhere near the thought of what would happen if the car started to move again. His arms were beginning to buckle under the weight of the door and that was with Dante taking half the burden. Eventually, he'd have to hold the thing alone.

Jacob heaved and strained his body across the chasm and clambered to the stairs. 'Just don't look down,' he said, as Kassia moved herself towards the gap.

'You can do it,' Jed encouraged.

'What if I can't?'

There was no way Jed could think about that possibility either.

It took Kassia less time than Jacob to negotiate the transfer. She snaked through the bars of the stair surround and then turned back to face them. Dante next. That meant Jed needed to take the whole weight of the hatch door. He braced his shoulders. His elbow throbbed and the gash on his hand reopened so that blood trickled down his arm.

Dante moved quickest of all. He cleared the distance between the elevator shaft and the stairs, tumbled through the bars, then turned.

Three faces stared at Jed from their place of safety. The hatch door bore down. Jed's legs wobbled. He was scared they'd give way. He had no idea how to keep the door raised and still negotiate the transfer to the stairs. But there was no time to plan. The elevator began to shake. The lights on the panel flashed. It was going to move again. If the elevator started to descend, Jed was too close to the opening! The movement would carry him forward and he'd be forced into the gulf between the shaft and the stairs and plummet to the ground. There was no time to work out the best way to do this. It just had to be done.

He flung one hand forward and grabbed the latticed metal bars about a metre away from him. As he swung, he released his other hand from beneath the rolling door. The sheet of metal slammed down like the blade of a guillotine behind him, grazing the back of his legs. He hauled his body close to the edge of the stairs and grabbed for the metal surrounds with his other hand. Fresh blood made his palm slippery. He could not grasp on. With only one hand, he hung on to the outside carcase of the stairs as the engine of the elevator whirred and spluttered and the car began to fall again.

Dante fumbled for Jed's other hand. With his eyes, Dante shouted not to let go. Jed gripped tightly, the blood oozing between his palm and Dante's. Kassia latched on to her brother, adding her weight to the effort to haul Jed upwards.

Red spots flickered in front of Jed's eyes. He couldn't hold on any longer. The hand gripping to the metal work was slipping too. He was going to fall. The air was whistling up from the ground, at least thirty metres below them.

Dante made a sound like a bear growling. He wrenched his arm back and suddenly Jed was through the bars and on the stairs.

Jed pressed his face for a moment against the steps and tried to let his breath regulate in his throat. But with his ear to the wood he could hear every movement from above. Footsteps. Racing down the stairs. And getting closer.

Jed remembered the escape from The Shard. This was worse. The stairs corkscrewed down the Petřín Tower so each tread was uneven. All four of them stumbled as they ran, arms banging against the metal bars that hemmed them in. Their footsteps thundered too now, so it was impossible to tell how close behind them Cole and Victor were. Jed pumped his arms as he hurtled downwards. Dante, Jacob and Kassia were doing their best to keep up.

Except, Jacob was struggling. His pace slowing on the uneven treads; the distance between him and

Kassia widening. 'Come on!' yelled Jed.

The bottom of the stairs opened into a lobby. There was a gift shop and a couple of ticket kiosks, all still closed. Jed charged towards the exit. The door was locked. He pummelled his fists against it but there was no give. Kassia peeled off from the others and ran back towards the door they'd come through. It was still ajar. She flung it wide open and Jed, Dante and Jacob crashed out after her, into the deserted forecourt of Petřín Gardens. Jed could hear running in the lobby. He grabbed Kassia's hand and raced towards a small wooden building to the left of the tower. They needed time to hide. To get their breath back and regroup.

The door to the Petřín Mirror Maze was open. Jed careered inside as the others followed.

He felt as if he'd been dropped inside the inner workings of a kaleidoscope. The space was filled with huge plaster archways, set at angles, each of them fronted with floor to ceiling polished mirrors. Bouncing back at them were their own reflections, duplicated over and over so that Jed saw himself a hundred times.

'Keep moving,' he yelled. And the replicated versions of those who were with him moved onwards too, a virtual army striving towards the centre of the maze.

The glass panels were as clear as mountain-river water. Night cleaners had left them sparkling. There were no smudged handprints to break the illusion and reveal what was real and what was reflection. Jed's mind was spinning. Not with the tail-eating dragon this time, but with confusion. Originals and replicas were indistinguishable. He tried to grab Kassia and pull her onwards but his fingers bounced against her glass imitation. Blood from his palm smeared a trail like breadcrumbs in a forest. Kassia darted ahead of him, several versions of herself turning to urge him ahead. But then behind him, or maybe in front of him, he couldn't tell because of the refection, he saw a flash of green clothing. Victor and Cole were in the maze.

Jed ran to the left. He stood still, trying to swallow the breath that was bubbling in his chest. Gasps of air misted the mirror in front of him and he wanted to reach out and wipe all trace of being there away. But moving towards the mirror would make him infinitely visible.

Cole and Victor were advancing together. Their images reflected and merged, a never-ending circle, and Jed knew that, at any moment, he would be sucked inside. He ducked down. Kassia was to his right, hidden too, by the twisting angle of the mirrors, but if either of them stepped forward, light would magnify their presence and their hiding place would be revealed.

Staying still was not an option. The route to the left was blocked. A dead end to the glass labyrinth. If they stayed where they were, both he and Kassia would be trapped.

Jed grabbed Kassia's hand and pitched headfirst, away from the dead end. A fan of replicas spanned out from the glass, bouncing against each other in an endless line.

But Jed wasn't fast enough. Cole saw the flash of movement and a hundred versions of him blocked their path.

Cole's eyes bored directly into Jed's. His arms wide, as they'd been at the top of the tower, ready to lock his hands around his prey. Jed cowered backwards. Cole's hands made contact, but with a mirage. The mirror shook on its frame. The polished glass buckled and shattered. A hundred reflected Jeds exploded into shafts of light. The real Jed ploughed straight on as Cole screamed out in frustration.

Red curtains marked the centre of the maze. Jed was alone now. He had no idea where Kassia or the others had gone. He could hear panting, choking breath. All he could see were versions of himself, disfigured now because of the shattered mirrors back in the network of reflections.

Suddenly, the red curtains surged up like waves on a stormy ocean and wrapped around him. He dropped to the ground, wrestling to be free, tugging and twisting as the curtains tightened, hemming him in. Through the gaps in the fabric shroud, he could see Victor, his eyes wild. Jed had escaped the clutches of this boy twice before and there was no way Victor would be defeated again.

Yet suddenly, behind Victor, Jed saw Kassia infinitely copied, a fire extinguisher raised like a trophy high above her head. She charged towards them and rammed the extinguisher hard into the closest mirror. The glass detonated like a bomb, spraying shards of shattered glass down on them like rain.

Victor covered his head to protect himself and in the confusion, Jed broke free of his curtained captivity and raced to the left.

In this second section of the maze, the mirrors formed an avenue funnelling towards a light. But the polished glass of these mirrors was puckered and bulged. The reflections they returned were stretched and then squashed versions of those who ran past them. Grotesque, huge-headed beasts: faces puffed, mouths pulled and eyes twisted. Jed raced past changed and monstrous versions of himself as he sprinted towards the light at the end of the tunnel. The exit was in reach but he could hear running behind him.

He shoulder-charged the door and tumbled through.

Dante and Kassia pulled him outside. Jacob followed, doubled over as he tried to catch his breath.

Back on the forecourt, there was no time to check for injuries. They had only one option left now and all four of them knew it.

If they had any chance of escape, they needed to take the train back down the hillside.

They charged across the gardens to the station, jumping over Cole's discarded spade as they ran. Jed didn't look back. Cole and Victor must be out of the maze by now but there was no sign of them.

The station was deserted. Jed clambered into the waiting carriage and Dante, Kassia and Jacob tumbled in behind him.

Jed's head was pulsing. He could hardly breathe. But he knew he had to start the train.

A radio intercom hung in the corner: a mouthpiece connected to a long, coiled cord. A dashboard of buttons was fixed to a raised metal board just below the front windscreen. And that was it. No wheel to steer a vehicle whose only job was to go forwards and back. One button was larger than the others. It was red. The ignition perhaps?

Jed looked at Dante, who widened his eyes and nodded.

Victor and Cole couldn't be far behind. He had to get this thing started.

'Brace yourselves,' yelled Jed. And he punched the red button.

Nothing.

Jed looked across at Dante.

He punched the button again.

Still nothing.

There had to be a security lock. Supposing someone fell against the dashboard and started the train by mistake.

Jed ran his hands along the underside edge of the raised control plate. His hand hit metal. A key. Andel must have left it there earlier.

Jed turned it sharply to the left. Then he punched the red button for a third time.

There was a thrumming noise. Blue lights ignited on the dashboard. An orange beacon began to turn and spin on the station. And the train began to move.

Jed allowed himself to breathe. The air was stuttering in his mouth. But he was OK. They were *all* OK. The train was moving down the hill and Victor and Cole were still nowhere to be seen.

Dante grabbed Jed and hugged him. It was going to be all right.

Jed looked back at Kassia and Jacob. They'd done it. They'd got away.

And as the train slid gracefully down the hillside, Jed really believed it.

Until he saw the bridge that spanned the track. Victor and Cole were standing on the edge. Both focused down on the train.

There was a moment of darkness as the train moved under the bridge. Then the sound of thunder.

The carriage emerged from the gloom and Jed glanced back. The bridge was empty.

Jed stared at Kassia. Fear had creased her face and terror flickered in her eyes.

But there was no more noise from above. The only sound Jed could hear was his heart thumping in his chest and the gentle hum of the cable as it pulled the train towards the bottom of the hill.

Maybe the men had seen the train passing under the bridge and realised it was over. Maybe things would still be OK.

Kassia was shaking. Dante clutched to the handrail. Jacob stood totally unmoved.

Silence.

Then the air exploded with the sound of breaking glass.

Victor and Cole were hanging on the outside of the

train, feet kicking against the shattered windows.

Jed and Dante wrestled with Cole's legs but the man was clinging hard to the roof, his feet windmilling, as he tried to get inside the carriage. There was a moment when Jed's face was so close to Cole's, he could see the whites of his eyes. The man was strong, his legs pummelling forward. Jed's hand was jerked free and Cole's boot whacked him sharply in the ribs. Jed staggered backwards in the carriage, crumpling against the metal handrail. Dante still clung on, and, for a moment, more of Cole's body was inside the train than outside. But Cole's hands were slipping. One skidded free of the roof, flailing frantically, trying to lock his fingers on air. He could not hold on.

And there was a moment of decision. Jed saw it in his eyes.

Cole twisted away from the train, bracing himself for the fall. He tumbled and rolled on the grass as he roared with anger at the train speeding on.

There was a second of relief. A beautiful moment of understanding that Cole could no longer hurt them. Then Jed turned.

Victor was standing in the carriage.

He brandished a spade like a weapon above his head.

The shaft of the spade whistled behind Jed, catching

on the intercom wire and pulling the receiver free of the cradle. The blade clanged against the dashboard. From his crouched position on the floor, Jed could see Kassia and Jacob huddled in the furthest corner of the carriage. Was one of them hurt? Was Kassia OK?

The spade swung again behind him. As Jed dived sideways, the blade banged down on the metal handrail, its reverberation echoing.

Jed turned again to look at Kassia. If Victor had hurt her . . . If, in this madness, she was injured . . .

Jed pushed hard against the floor of the moving carriage. He couldn't let it happen! He would not allow this boy to take everything from him that he valued most. A wave of energy surged through his body and he felt himself changing; becoming like the distorted beast from the mirror maze, twisted and consumed with rage.

Jed threw himself at Victor, grabbing his legs. The boy staggered, lost his balance and fell, his body slamming hard against the floor, the spade clattering from his hands.

Through the shattered window, Jed could see the counterbalanced train moving up the hill towards them. Within moments it would be in reaching distance. If the others could make it on to the second carriage they would be free.

15th August 1951

...s qui bouillaient dans une c...
...e, la fille de l'empereur m'a...
...voyais plus clairement que l'h...
...e cour; ils me paraissaient plus...
...u jardin vers la cime duquel je...

...s, leurs griffes aigues, les langues c...
...ueule me déchiraient les oreilles ou...
...d et brûlaient mes joues. Ma pauvre...
...dormais, se réveillait, mais en vain ell...
...t me caressait, me donnant à boire. Les...
...oyais rien, n'entendais rien et mes joues re...
...'à me faire mal, comme si elles avaie...
braise.
...s par mes rires qu'à minuit je réveilla...
...er m'apparaissait la jeune fille du laurier...
...cadette de l'empereur et la bor...
...er le beau prince par la vallée des larm...
...orte de son premier milieu, non seulem...
...une certaine façon anormale d'être. Il in...
...ité; cette réalité, il la transforme et il l'au...
...es comme celle qui présente la mort de...
...illusions terribles qu'il a au milieu de...
...at est entré dans la chambre, parce qu'u...
...parce qu'il y a eu un bruit dans la cour,...
...te ressuscite.
...bre nuit! A sa tête brûlait un cierge...
...oisées sur la poitrine. Le père était par...
...pain quotidien, sans donner de nouve...
...nt endormis en pleurant.
...i doucement, comme un chat, et m'agen...
...à elle. Je restai comme pétrifié en pensa...
...a envoyé en rêve la nouvelle de cela,...
...lque part et, si je me presserai, je pourr...
...r... Mes pensées furent interrompues pa...
...les draps de la morte. Je saillis debout. Je m'incli...
...Un bruit de planches. Je tressaillis. Ma chérie se...

'Get out! The other train!' Jed yelled.

Somehow, Dante needed no words to understand the plan. He dragged Kassia towards the shattered window, crouching with her on the sill as the second carriage pulled closer. Jacob scrambled up beside them.

'What about you?' screamed Kassia, straining towards Jed.

But Victor was beginning to come round. His shoulders were heaving; his body rising like a creature from a swamp.

'Jed!'

'Go!' Jed screamed. He grabbed for the fallen intercom and lassoed the coiled wire round Victor's shoulders. Victor was standing now, the wire tight around him. He tried to pull the wire free but Jed held fast. This boy had ruined everything. They'd been so close. And now all hope of answers was lost.

Victor's hands scrabbled with the wire. He tugged it free of his shoulders but Jed yanked hard. The wire was at Victor's throat.

And in that second, time slowed: the moment ballooned in perfect clarity.

Victor's face was angled to the side, his hands grappling at the wire. His eyes met Jed's.

This boy had been there. At the Neckar.

Kassia's voice sliced the air. 'Jed, please!' She

reached out her hand.

But he'd also been at The Shard, where he'd opened the cage and let Jed free.

Jed's fingers stung as if they'd been burnt. He let go of the wire and Victor spluttered and stumbled, sinking to his knees.

Jed grabbed Kassia's hand and climbed up on to the window opening. The second carriage was directly beside them.

They jumped.

Jed's fingers scrabbled to catch hold of the roof. Climbing inside the train was not an option. The windows were closed. Kassia floundered beside him, one hand unable to catch the roof. They pressed their bodies against the outside of the train and the carriage pulled up the hill.

Jed's heart was pounding in his chest.

'I thought you were going to . . . I thought . . .' Kassia's voice was coming in gulping spurts like blood spouting from an open wound.

He didn't want to know what she thought. He didn't want to think about what had happened in the other carriage. And he didn't want to think about the bridge just ahead of them on the track, getting nearer every second.

There would not be room. The side of the carriage

ran so close to the brickwork, they would be squashed between the wall and the train as they clung to the outside.

Dante kicked the carriage with his foot and the metal pulsed with urgency. But there was no time left to break the windows. No sign language was necessary now to explain the only option left to them.

Jed took a deep breath and looked across at Kassia. 'Ready?' he said with his eyes.

She nodded.

As one, the four let go of the side of the carriage and somersaulted into the grass and the overgrowth, rolling and rolling as the train hurtled through the tunnel and disappeared.

Jed took a moment to check that no parts of him were broken. He was winded, his chest had hit the ground first as he'd fallen from the train, but otherwise he was unhurt. He pulled himself up and looked for the others.

Kassia and Jacob had rolled further down the hill and were both on their knees now, shakily pushing themselves to stand. But Dante had tumbled even further and was struggling to get to his feet.

Jed hurried through the undergrowth to him.

Dante had injured his ankle in the fall and was

gingerly trying to press his foot to the ground. Jed and Kassia linked arms either side of him to try and help him walk. This made it possible for him to move forwards but impossible for him to talk to them about how much pain he was in – though his groans made it pretty clear.

'We need to get away from the train track,' Jed said urgently.

'We need to check his ankle,' hissed Kassia, with equal desperation.

They compromised and forced their way over the uneven ground towards a building which was hidden in the trees.

It was a church made entirely of wood. An eccentric design of turrets and towers that looked as if it had been dropped into Petřín Park and then abandoned. The door was locked but there was a wide overhanging covered porch.

Carefully, Jed and Kassia lowered Dante to the floor.

His ankle was swollen and puffy, but despite the pain, he could move the foot and so it seemed likely no bones were broken. Jacob rolled up their coats and jackets and stuffed them as a cushion under Dante's heel.

'What do we do?'

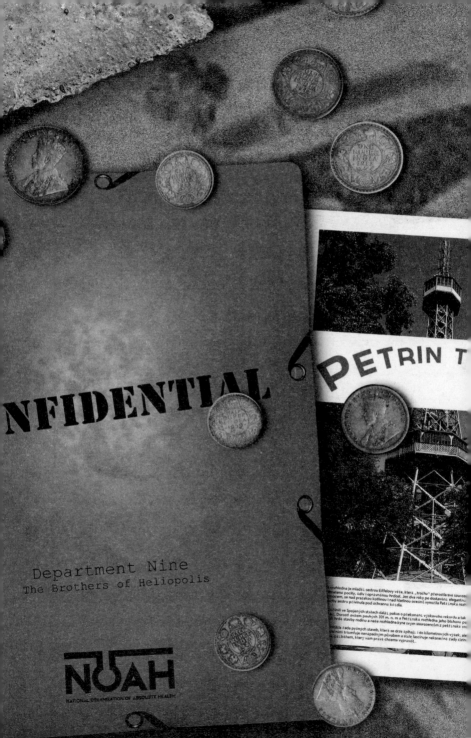

Kassia's question seemed almost laughable. Shouldn't they talk about how NOAH had found them? Shouldn't they chat about how they hadn't got the recipe? Shouldn't they at least mention that they'd nearly all been killed?

And then Jed did laugh. Because nothing made sense, least of all the idea of an immortal nearly dying.

He covered his mouth in shame but Kassia was laughing too. 'Nice visit to the tower, was it?' she blurted. 'Oh yes, lovely time. Everyone should do it. I particularly liked the mirror maze. Had a cracking time in there!'

'I liked the train best,' joined in Jacob. 'You can choose to travel inside the carriage, on the roof or on the side. Lovely view of the gardens!'

Dante smiled too. 'Did you buy a souvenir fridge magnet?' he signed. 'Oh no. I got myself a busted ankle. You?'

'No. I went for lacerations of the arm,' said Jed, turning his shoulder to flick away tiny shards of glass. 'Thought they'd go with my severed palm.'

Kassia giggled. Then she bit her lip in an attempt to gain control. 'Seriously. What do we do now?'

Eventually, the plan was simple. The chances of Cole and Victor finding them in the hidden church was small but not impossible, so they'd stay for a while just to rest and make sure Dante was well enough to move on. Jacob would try and find them something to eat and they'd take it in turns to catch a few moments of sleep. They'd been awake for over twenty-four hours and they had to get their strength back. At dusk, they'd try and get back into central Prague. Then the station. Then out of the city.

That was it. No one talked about the elixir. It was the unspoken cloud that settled round them like the fragments of glass that glinted on their clothes and in their hair.

And like a shard of glass, the thought of not finding the recipe wormed its way into Jed's blood and pulsed around him.

'How did you let him get away? *Again!*' Cole was spitting his words as he tried to bandage the gaping cut on his arm. He'd pulled a sliver of glass from his bicep and the blood was spewing on to the tattooed unicorn.

'This is not my fault!' yelled Victor. 'And that boy tried to kill me.' Victor reached up to his neck. It was still raw from where the intercom lead had dug into his skin.

But Fulcanelli hadn't killed him. He could have done. There'd been a moment, just as the girl had called to him, when Victor had seen something flash in the boy's eyes. Why had he stopped? They'd tried to drown him in the Neckar. They'd made him drink poison. They'd kept him in a cage. Victor remembered the cage. And he remembered the words Fulcanelli had used as he forced his way past to get free. He'd said 'I'm sorry.'

Victor rubbed his hand again across his neck. He didn't want to think about any of that now. What mattered was what they did next.

Cole gritted his teeth and pulled the ripped Czech flag he'd stolen from the station gift shop tighter around his arm.

It had taken the two of them nearly an hour to find each other. Cole had eventually returned to the bottom of Petřín Hill where Victor had decided it was best to wait. He figured if he hung around long enough, Fulcanelli and his friends would pass through the funicular station too. He'd last seen them on the train, and by that he meant quite literally *on* the train, travelling back towards the tower. But they hadn't returned. And by now they could be anywhere.

'Do we report this back to London?' said Victor.

Cole shook his head. 'You have a death wish, do you?'

'So what do we do?'

Cole stood up. The tourniquet around his arm had slowed the bleeding, but the hooves of the chained unicorn were red now. 'We have to block the exit out of the city.'

'So, the main train station? Where will they go?'

'No idea. But if we close down their chances to leave Prague, then we don't need to worry.'

Victor wasn't sure about that. But he'd learned better than to share any of that concern with anyone at NOAH, least of all Cole Carter. He took his hand down from his neck and closed it around the small dog-eared photograph he kept inside his pocket. 'Let's get moving,' he said.

Jacob returned to St Michael's church with a selection of snacks to keep them going. Kassia devoured the chlebíčky, which looked like a large open sandwich. It was garnished with a rather too-generous helping of pickled cucumber, if she was really honest, but she was so hungry she ate it all anyway and washed it down with kofola. She finished her meal with a portion of křížaly which, Jacob assured her, were chips of dried apple, although they looked more like pencil sharpenings.

Food was not their only problem. They needed a plan to get them out of Prague as quickly as possible, so once everyone had eaten, they discussed all the possibilities.

Taking a night train seemed the best idea. They'd get as far away as they could from the city and have a proper chance to sleep. No one had managed more than a few minutes napping in the covered porch of the church. It didn't even matter where they took the train to. Just as far away from Prague as they could get, so they could think about what they needed to do next. Budapest seemed a long way, so they settled on there.

They'd brought no extra clothes with them to Prague so they needed to buy provisions. There'd been plenty of shops at the station but everyone agreed they should spend as little time there as possible. NOAH was bound to have people posted waiting for them. That left the idea of shopping for basic supplies in the most touristy part of the city where they could get lost in the crowds of holiday makers.

It seemed a risky plan to Kassia. But nothing anyone suggested seemed without risk. So it was agreed.

Dante could bear weight on his ankle as long as they walked slowly, and it took them about an hour to get to the road that ran along the bottom of Petřín Park. They boarded a tram that travelled across the Vltava and into the Old Town. The light was fading.

And Kassia was scared. But they had no choice.

Jed rested his head against the window as the tram juddered past the Old Jewish Cemetery.

'What happened in the train carriage?' Kassia said quietly. 'With Victor? And the wire?'

'You thought I was going to kill him?' Jed's face looked so sad she was scared to answer.

'Would you have done?'

Jed turned in his seat. 'Kassia, I thought he was going to hurt you. Thought he *had* hurt you.'

'And you would have killed him?'

Jed turned his face away again. It was getting dark and the roads outside were slipping past in an inky gloom.

Kassia knew better than to push it. 'Do you think Andel really did have the recipe?' she asked.

'We'll never know now.'

Jed kept his eyes on the road and Kassia said no more until Jacob tapped her on the shoulder and gestured for them to get off at the next stop.

The sky was thickening with cloud. It was cold and a wind was blowing in from the river. 'Let's get this done quickly,' said Jacob.

They bought T-shirts and jeans, a support bandage for Dante's ankle and some painkillers, bottles of water and snacks, as well as a map of Europe and a guide to the night-train service.

What they really should have bought were umbrellas.

By the time they had everything they needed, it was as if the clouds had sunk too close to the turrets and spires of the city and been lanced like giant balloons. Kassia had never felt rain like it.

'We need to shelter somewhere,' signed Dante. 'The train to Budapest doesn't leave until nearly midnight.'

'So a restaurant maybe?' said Jacob.

'Too risky,' said Jed. 'We'd be like sitting ducks, waiting to be seen.'

'So where?' quipped Jacob, his annoyance at his rejected plan so obvious Kassia felt a little awkward.

They'd passed a synagogue a few blocks back but the rain was so heavy that everything they'd bought would be soaked unless they got inside quickly. She looked across to the right at a parade of small boutiques and expensive gift shops. A blue door was propped open and some delivery men were unloading boxes from the back of a white transit van that had parked up on the cobbled walkway.

Kassia turned in the shop's direction. 'There.'

Jed pulled a face. 'Why?' It was obvious he hadn't seen what she'd seen.

But for Kassia the idea of hiding anywhere else now

seemed ridiculous. 'The sign,' she urged. 'Look!'

She pointed to the blue door and the wooden logo hanging above it, spelling out that this was not another boutique or souvenir shop.

Jed's smile was the first one she'd seen since they'd been sitting on the church porch. 'Perfect!' he said. 'But how do we get inside without being noticed?'

Kassia came up with the plan.

She approached the delivery men on her own, flapping a rather soggy map of Prague. She spoke loudly and slowly, dropping in the occasional word in Czech, as if she was attempting to ask directions. The delivery men were at first annoyed to be disturbed. They had goods to drop off, a schedule to keep. And it was pouring with rain. But Kassia's impression of a lost and anxious tourist would have left only the most stony-hearted unmoved.

While the two delivery men gestured up towards the Old Town centre and pointed out locations on the map, Dante, supported by Jed and Jacob, hobbled through the open blue door behind them. The three of them hid in the foyer and were still hiding there when, minutes later, the delivery men carried the last boxes in, slammed the door and clambered back into their van.

Kassia strode down the street until she heard the

chug of the van's engine. She waved cheerfully as it drove past her, mouthing the words 'thank you' again as it passed. Then she turned and ran back to the blue doorway.

She thumped three times and Jed opened the door ever so slightly to check that it was her. Then he ushered her inside. 'Welcome to Prague's Museum of Alchemy,' he said.

Kassia tripped over the edge of a box that had been left in the foyer, and grinned apologetically. Rain dripped from her hair and shoulders and puddled on to the floor.

Jed steered her away from the re-bolted door and stood beside her as she looked around.

He guessed the space they stood in had once served as an entrance hall when the museum had been used as a house. A particularly nice house, he thought to himself. The floor was intricately tiled and plaster walls were lined with shelves. These were stacked with books and brightly coloured bottles of all shapes and sizes. The domed ceiling was high above them, and painted in each of the four corners were single words. He whispered each one to himself. He was pretty sure he recognised them. *Terra*. That meant earth. *Ignis*. Fire. So the four words probably stood for the four elements:

earth, fire, water and air. Something about these words made him feel warm. The fact that he was still soaked from the rain no longer seemed important.

Hanging down from the ceiling were bunches of flowers. This was perhaps why the space smelt so beautiful. *Not* so beautiful was the chandelier in the centre of the ceiling. It was a basic circle of wood decorated with three enormous metal heads. Each head had horns and was staring down sinisterly. There was something familiar about these too but this time Jed felt less comfortable. He couldn't tell if the heads were supposed to be goats, but they reminded him of the devil.

'Is this really a museum?' Kassia said from beside him.

'I think that's pushing it,' signed Dante mockingly. 'Looks more like a gift shop trying to cash in on the city's links to alchemy. Who buys this sort of stuff?' He passed her a small glass bottle filled with sparkling crimson liquid. There was a neat hand-written label, which helpfully translated the contents using several languages.

'Love potion,' said Kassia, twisting the label with her slightly wet fingers. 'Nice.'

'Expensive,' said Jacob.

Bundles of dried flowers fanned out from baskets in

front of the shelves. Kassia looked at the price and took a sharp intake of breath. 'Tourists like this sort of thing. Authentic Prague.'

'Yeah, well maybe they do. But the place shouldn't claim to be a museum,' said Jed. 'It's just a shop.'

He moved over to a bookcase set into a recess on the wall. It was piled with books and postcards, all priced for purchase, but amongst the sale goods were props best suited for a film about ancient magic. A flamboyant feather quill was propped inside a decorated stone ink pot. A string of beads twisted round the base. But the item to the left of that was the one which made Jed falter a little and step in closer.

The wooden statue was of a dragon. It was seated, its head straining upwards, its tail curled like the string of beads around its feet. The wood shone in the light; a soft warm glow. It looked to Jed as if, at any moment, the dragon would uncoil its tail, stretch and take a yawn.

The odd thing was, this thought didn't scare him.

There was no spinning. No boring down into his memory. Just a wooden dragon on a bookshelf, among lots of other tourist goodies waiting to be bought.

Jed put his hand on the dragon's head and tried to lift it. Wow it was heavy. The thing was fixed firmly to the shelf. He twitched his fingers and twisted the dragon as if trying to unscrew a lid from a bottle. The dragon turned on the shelf, spinning a fraction. It did not rise.

But there was a gentle click.

Jed went to pull his hand away. But the whole shelf unit had begun to move backwards into the recess. He held firmly to the wooden dragon. Another click and then the shelf unit slid to the side revealing an open archway. 'What the . . . ?'

Kassia was behind him. 'What did you do? How did you open that?'

'The dragon!' said Jed. 'It's a secret doorway. What do you think's down there?'

Jacob was behind them too. 'No idea, mate. But I think we're about to find out.'

It was dark beyond the door. The light from the foyer failed to spill through the secret opening and so it was impossible to see what was there. Jed reached out his hands to steady himself against the stone walls and his fingers caught on some sort of fixing. He felt upwards. An old-fashioned torch. He lifted it out of the holding. A metal baton topped with some sort of baled hay, wrapped in linen. 'Great lighting system. Anyone got a match?'

Jacob pushed forward to stand beside him and fiddled with the underneath of the wall fixing. There was a click and then he held out a small box in his hands.

Jed was impressed.

'Logic,' said Jacob. 'Keep what you need close to where you need it.'

Jed struck a match and held it towards the torch. It took a moment, but then the baled linen began to glow. It sent an arc of warm light forward, sliding up the walls and across the floor in front of them. And now it was clear to see that the floor fell away and became a twisting staircase.

'Ready?' said Jed, holding the torch in front of him.

He guessed the movement of the others as they shuffled to be closer to him showed that they were.

Jed led the way. The stairs were rough stone, scooped down in the middle of each tread as if years of footfall had worked like water against rock, wearing away at the surface. As they corkscrewed down, the air became colder. It was damp and stale. It reminded Jed of the smell of stagnant river water and he shivered. There was no handrail and so he steadied himself as he descended, fingers brushing against the walls, which were worn away too in places, as if others had reached out for security through centuries of descents.

At the bottom of the stairs, they entered a low-ceilinged corridor. Jed bent his head a little and the light from the torch danced like flame ghosts on the walls. The corridor curved slightly to the left, the ceiling becoming ever lower. Jed stooped even more, his shoulders rounded.

Eventually, the corridor ended and opened out into a sort of underground crossroads. Through the torchlight, it was possible to see that signs had been tacked to the stonework to guide visitors across the junction. Jed couldn't read them, but one looked like the word he'd seen used in the city above, on signs pointing towards the 'castle'. Perhaps the tunnels gave access to all parts of Prague, like some vast subterranean network of secret access. The thought was exciting.

The fourth opening at the crossroads was unsigned and slightly wider than the other three. More of an entrance than a continuation of the tunnel system. 'Shall I?' Jed called over his shoulder. But it was a statement of intent rather than a real question. Something was drawing him forward, deeper into the underground cavern.

The footsteps of those behind him echoed on the stone as they followed him.

The wider tunnel they'd followed opened up at last into a wide, square space like a room.

'Wow.' Jed held the torch up higher so the flames nearly caught against the low hanging ceiling. The orange light spilled into every corner. 'This place is incredible.'

The room seemed to be divided into three main sections beyond the opening of the entrance. One wall was lined with wooden shelving which jutted out of the stone, some of it sloping awkwardly, as if the shelves had tried for years to remain straight but had finally relented and relaxed, their ends bowing down towards the ground. On the shelves were all sorts of metal instruments, bottles and containers. Candles sat unlit, pressed into pottery bases and leather rags wrapped around small, squat, glass vessels that were veiled in dust. Bunches of dried flowers spilled from the uneven shelving, their colours bleached by time, so they looked more like sheaves of browned corn than floral arrangements. On the highest shelf, in the corner, was a human skull. The light from the torch filled the empty eye sockets. It looked as if the skull was watching them; not surprised by their appearance, more that it had been expecting them.

In the second section of the room, some sort of oven or kiln had been built into the brickwork. On overhanging stone shelves, there were rows of pottery containers. All were sized differently but the basic shape of each was the same. A narrow, stout-necked bottle that widened out to a fuller base. On the front of each container there was a tapered spout that stretched down, often beyond the base of the container itself. It meant the spouts had to overhang the shelving, making it look like the containers were statues of oddly formed people sitting and allowing one single leg to hang playfully down.

The final section of the room housed a large wooden table. There were wooden stalls around it, and larger clay structures like capped chimneys circled it, almost like a protective ring. On the wall behind the table, there was a metal plaque set into the brick and on a lip of stone just above the plaque there were five cracked and broken bottles. Above this was a small painted portrait of a man.

'What is this place?' gasped Kassia.

'I reckon it's some sort of alchemical lab,' said Jed, sweeping the torch in front of him so that the eye sockets of the human skull suddenly grew dark. Kassia signed his answer for Dante.

'So who's that guy?' said Jacob, pointing up at the portrait.

Kassia drummed her fingers against her lips as if she was scanning her memory, trying to recall all the images she'd seen in the books they'd searched through and the websites they'd accessed when trying to make connections. 'Rudolph, maybe?' she guessed aloud.

'He was the emperor who was so into alchemy. He's the guy who called all the alchemists to Prague.'

'And tested them when they came,' added Jacob. 'House of the Stone Ram, and all that.'

'And so they ended up working here,' said Jed, moving the torch again so the skull eye sockets danced once more with light from the flame. 'Kind of strange to imagine.'

Jed ran his fingers across the closest pottery container, its slender spout stretching downwards. He felt an odd tingle in his fingers. But it was not unpleasant or painful. He did not pull his hand away.

'They made elixirs here?' said Jacob, turning the phrase into a question. 'Love potions like the things they sell upstairs?'

Jed let his hand slide free of the container and for a moment he felt weirdly empty. He walked across the space to the metal plaque on the wall. The torchlight illuminated the five cracked and broken bottles and it looked for just a second as if each one was filled with golden liquid.

Jed heard a ringing in his ears. A soft buzzing. And then slowly, and almost gracefully, the image of the six-segmented dragon began to spin in front of his eyes.

But there was no pain or repulsion connected to the memory.

For the first time since Jed had seen the spinning dragon, it turned and turned in such a way that he didn't want to close his eyes and shut it out. He saw the dragon, golden and glinting, rainbow-coloured scales overlapping in an intricate skin. He watched as it twisted and turned, the space in the centre of the circle it made filled not with images of horror or pain. Instead, the space was filled with a bright, pulsating light. And it was beautiful.

Jed felt a surge of heat pulsing out from the centre of his body and filling every fibre. And he breathed in deeply, not wanting the warmth ever to end.

Suddenly, he was aware of voices. Kassia and Dante were reaching out for his arms. Jacob had taken the torch from his hand. And the three of them were staring at him.

'Are you OK? Another bad memory?' said Kassia urgently.

Jed shook his head. Not bad. The most beautiful memory he'd had.

Kassia's face was screwed up in concentration. 'Jed?'

He turned and looked again, around the space they'd found. And the air no longer smelt like stagnant water. It felt full of excitement and promise.

'They worked down here,' he said slowly, as if his voice was new and untested. 'The alchemists from the past. Working in secret to try and find the elixir. And look at all the things they kept.' He rubbed his face as if suddenly he could see things more clearly. The ghostly trace of the dragon spun one more time behind his eyes and then drifted away like pollen being blown from flowers on a summer day. 'I don't think he destroyed it,' he said quietly.

'Who? Destroyed what?' asked Kassia.

'Canseliet,' said Jed.

The others peered at him in the flickering light of the torch.

'The third book the librarian told us about.'

He guessed the others were thinking back to the tower of infinite books on the steps of the library. But Jed's mind was stretching further.

'It made total sense about me not writing down the recipe in the two published books. Public domain and all that. But supposing the third book, the one that was never published, had the recipe in it?'

He could see the others were trying desperately to keep up.

'We know the Brothers of Heliopolis worked together, right. And if they found the recipe for the elixir of life, and I wrote it down in the third book and

Canseliet had it, then there's no way he would destroy it. It's like Andel and our chase around the city. It was all a trick. A delaying tactic to keep us here until NOAH could find us.'

It was clear from the way that the others were looking at him that he was making no sense.

'Look at this place. Alchemists working in secret for centuries. Of course if they found the recipe for the elixir of life they'd keep it secret. And putting out a story that Fulcanelli's greatest work was destroyed is just a cover. They gave up so much to do this. People thought alchemists were nutters and frauds. I just don't think Canseliet would have done it.'

'You think Fulcanelli's third book is still out there?' Kassia signed slowly.

'Yes!' And Jed was sure. 'Andel tricked us. And the stuff about Canseliet is a trick too!'

'But what makes you think the third book has the recipe in it?'

'Fulcanelli's great work, was what the librarian called it. What could be greater than making the elixir of life? And of course, saying the recipe was destroyed makes sense. But it doesn't make it true!'

'So where do we find the third book?'

Jed began to pace. The fire from the memory and the torch seemed to be pulsing through his veins.

'I can't unravel it all, but there're things that are important. Stone books, right. That has to mean something.'

'But we've searched the stone books!'

'Of Prague. But there could be others.' He was agitated. His synapses sparking. He'd never felt more alive.

Kassia was struggling to keep up with the signs needed to help Dante stay in the loop. Jed had lost all sense of how to make words with his hands. His fingers were twitching, as if he was trying to grab hold of something that was just out of reach.

'What were my other books called?'

'Erm. *The Mystery of the Cathedrals* and *Dwellings of the Philosophers*,' said Kassia.

'And the third one. The lost one, with the recipe?'

'Something about Glory. *Finis Gloriae Mundi* I think. The librarian said it meant *End of the World's Glory*.'

Jed ran the titles around in his head. Cathedrals. Dwellings. Glory. Then other words that bubbled in his mind like boiling liquid. Elixirs. Recipes. Underground laboratories. 'That's it!' He stood stock-still.

Everyone looked at him. The torch flickered.

'Dwellings. Cathedrals. Glory. I get it now.

Reverend Cockren said that St Paul's was like a great picture book of signs, remember! It's a stone book just like Prague!'

'You think the recipe for the elixir of life is back at St Paul's?' urged Jacob.

'No!'

'But you *know* where it is?'

Jed nodded. 'I think I do.'

Victor looked up at the departure board as Cole strode backwards and forwards behind him. They'd collected their coats and bags from the House of the Stone Ram and Cole had paid off Andel for his help. He'd given him half of what NOAH had agreed. Cole said he was lucky to get even that. And they'd been at the station for hours, scanning the crowds and watching the electronic screens click and change like the most boring television show Victor had ever been unfortunate enough to watch. Surveillance, he decided, was not his thing.

'Where would you go?' Victor called over his shoulder. 'If you were running away?'

Cole was pacing beside him, his turn now to fix his focus on the crowds. He stopped for a moment and blew a bubble with the piece of gum he was chewing. 'I wouldn't be running away.'

Victor shrugged. Maybe Cole had never thought about it. But up until a few months ago, running away was all that Victor had ever thought about. Getting clear of Etkin House. That was all he'd wanted. The problem had been – and he'd given this lots of thought while lying on his bed and staring at a map of the constellations – that he'd had nowhere to run to.

'I mean, they can go anywhere they want. Look at all these destinations,' he said. There was a complicated grid of connecting stops and eventual destinations and it looked to Victor as if someone had taken a thick red marker pen and scribbled over a map of Europe. 'Budapest. Vienna. Amsterdam. Cologne. How are we supposed to guess?'

Cole blew another bubble. It snapped as it popped on his tongue. 'So where would you go?'

Victor shook his head. There'd been nowhere. But he guessed he knew where he wanted it to be. 'Home,' he said quietly.

'Say again.'

'That's where I'd go. If I had a proper one. Home.'

Cole pulled a face. 'You reckon they'll make tracks back to London?'

'Not *her* home. His.'

'Oh.' Cole was weighing Victor's words.

'Hey. Don't worry about it. I was just thinking out

loud.' Victor ran his finger down the edge of the photograph inside his pocket.

But Cole was nodding. 'Come on.'

'Where are we going?'

Cole took the gum from his mouth and squeezed it inside the folds of an empty paper wrapper. 'Where you said. Come on.'

'Really? You don't want to wait and be sure?'

'There're too many people here.' He tossed the gum into the bin. 'We'll never find them unless we get tickets and commit to a platform. If you're wrong, then I'll deal with the consequences. But you *won't* be wrong.'

Victor was unnerved by Cole's confidence. Would a boy who could live for ever really think the same as him? Make the same decision? Wouldn't the world be bigger and more exciting, than just *home*? 'OK,' he said nervously. 'If you say so.'

Cole nodded and took another stick of gum and rolled it into his mouth. Then he led the way to the City-Night-Line departure platform, the train's destination carefully selected from the board.

# DAY 61
## 29th April

The sleeping compartment on the City-Night-Line train was called a couchette. It was tiny. There were two bunks on each side, one high and one low. There was a thin blue mattress on each one and a tiny pillow inside a case that looked like it was made of paper. Between the bunks was a small square window covered by a stiff yellow curtain. In front of that was a ladder fixed to the ceiling, which Kassia presumed was how you got up to the top sleeping space. There was no toilet. No wash basin. They'd paid for the most basic four-person compartment and that was what it was. Basic.

Dante dumped the bag on the floor. 'Seriously?' he signed. 'Could this be any smaller?'

'Yeah, well at least you won't get woken up by people snoring,' signed Kassia.

The space seemed awkwardly intimate, but the midnight train was heavily overbooked and it was either get tickets for the four-berth couchette or wait until the next night for a more expensive sleeper compartment. The agent had assured them that they were lucky to have a couchette just to themselves. If you booked single berths, then you had to share with strangers. He'd handed over their tickets, warned them about the tight transfer time in Cologne and then directed them to a train named *The Phoenix*. Kassia had been cheered a little by the name but all that positivity had drained away since boarding. They were on the run again. And she was exhausted.

Jed pressed the mattress with his hands and then beat the pillow vigorously in an attempt to plump it full of air. He looked agitated. The plumping of the pillow was going on much longer than Kassia thought necessary. 'You OK?' she said.

'More than OK,' he answered.

Somehow, this response troubled Kassia more than if he'd said no.

So much had happened in the last twenty-four hours. They'd been betrayed; had all their hopes for answers dashed and been nearly killed. But Jed looked more energised than she'd seen him since they'd been in London. Since before he knew who he was. He really believed the recipe was in reach this time and she could hardly bear to look at the hope that shone in his eyes. What would they do if he was wrong? What if he hadn't worked out the truth? What if all that was waiting for them was more disappointment? And what if this night-time journey across Europe was just another massive waste of time?

Jed had tried to disguise the tremors in his hand. He suggested the loss of strength on the chase around Prague was just because of the memories. But Kassia feared it was more than that. Every day was precious, and the race for the elixir was draining him. In moments when he didn't know she was watching him, she saw the lines deepen under his eyes from pain. He was dying. Immortal, but getting closer to death every single day. When she allowed herself to think about that for just a second, she felt so scared that she was sure her heart would forget to beat. She needed air and there was hardly any inside this tiny compartment.

'I need the toilet,' she signed bluntly. 'Need to freshen up a bit.'

Dante nodded and vaulted up the ladder and lay back on the top mattress, his hands behind his head, gazing up at the ceiling as if he was staring at a beautiful night sky sparked with stars.

'Don't be long,' said Jacob, sitting on the lower

bunk, and ducking to avoid the metal overhang.

Kassia smiled weakly and stepped outside into the corridor.

The train was moving so quickly it was difficult to walk. She steadied herself, shut the couchette door and turned right.

There was something reassuring about the steady rolling of the train as she walked. It comforted her and, after using the loo, she stood for a while in the corridor, her hands pressed against the cold glass of the windows. There was nothing to see. Light glinted in the distance but the darkness of night pressed in. She could have been anywhere in the world. She closed her eyes, leaned her forehead against the glass and sunk into the rhythm of the ride.

'You OK?' a voice came from behind her.

For a second she thought it was Jed. She wanted it to be him. Wanted him to have worried enough to come to find her. But the voice was laced with an accent and as she listened she realised the voice had spoken before, perhaps asking her in a different language first, if she was all right.

She turned round.

The speaker was a boy. Older than her. Very late teens, she guessed, or maybe early twenties. He was tall and willowy, his wrists encircled with coloured braids and leather bracelets, a leather choker with something that looked like a shark tooth tied tight in the hollow of his neck. His hair was black and untamed; long to his shoulders. And a single hoop earring hung from his left earlobe. His eyes were so dark they were almost as black as the night outside the window.

He asked the question again. In English. And Kassia mumbled a reply. 'I'm fine.'

'You is looking sad,' the boy said and it was such a bold and undisguised thing to say, Kassia was unsure how to answer. So she stared down at her feet.

'I'm Giseppi,' the boy said. 'Giseppi Bergier.' He thrust out his hand and the bracelets moved as one, rattling further down his wrist.

Kassia shook his hand awkwardly. 'Kassia Devaux,' she said.

'Ahh.' His face registered surprise. And maybe even something more than this. 'So you are French?'

'Family were. But not me.'

He seemed disappointed by that and he peered at her, as if he was as surprised by this answer as he was by her assertion that she was OK. 'I could paint the smile on your face,' he said, angling his head to the side and grinning down at her, his dark eyes sparking. 'It's what I do. Painting of the faces.'

Again she didn't know how to answer him, so she said nothing.

'I'm a clown,' he said, opening his hands wide as if this statement would explain everything.

'Really?' Did he mean he worked in a circus?

'Really.' He laughed and the sound was soft and soothing. 'I get the money to make the people happy. I like it.'

'Sounds fun,' she said.

'There's nothing more good.' He waited a bit. 'There is lots of us on board. Clowns, I mean.'

'Going on some sort of clown holiday?' she said.

'Sort of. We go to the Festival of Fools.'

'Oh.' Her answer was meaningless. She'd no idea what he was talking about, although a part of her brain seemed to be drifting back to a story she'd read not that long ago. She was too tired to fully place the memory.

'Once the train stops and we get ready with our connection, you'll be seeing lots of the clowns and the greasepaint and the wigs. You must prepare. '

Kassia was still struggling to connect to the mention of the Festival of Fools.

'Seriously. You look like the weight of the world is being on your shoulders,' Giseppi said quietly. 'You is sure you want not to tell me what's wrong?' He leant back on the door of the couchette behind him and folded his arms across his chest. 'I'm good with the listening and our paths will move away when the train ends. You will never see of me again. Secret are with me, very safe.'

Suddenly, Kassia was overwhelmed with an urge to tell him everything. About Jed. About her home burning down. About NOAH. To let all the details tumble out so she could lay them down in order like the sectioned track the train was pelting forwards on.

But she didn't. 'I'm just miles from home chasing a dream that might never come true,' she said. 'And there're people trying to stop me.'

'You is being the normal teenager then,' Giseppi said kindly.

Kassia folded her arms across her tummy and pressed in tight.

'Anyway,' he said, his eyes twinkling, 'if you decide to come then I make you the painted smile.' There was nothing artificial about the grin he gave her. 'You look like you could do with one.' He tapped his hand against the couchette door behind him. 'This is where I'll be if you need of me.'

'Thanks,' she said, and the smile she gave him felt genuine too. In fact, as Giseppi stepped into the couchette and closed the door behind him, Kassia felt more relaxed. She was cross with herself for being negative before. And the others were probably worrying about her.

She straightened herself up and took a deep breath.

She'd made a decision. She'd find the buffet car, take back some food and then start planning with everyone how exactly they'd find the recipe Jed was so sure was in Fulcanelli's third book. What had she got to be miserable about, after all? Yes, they were on the run. But they were at least running *towards* solutions.

Kassia pulled out a wad of crumpled euros from her pocket as she made her way down the train in the direction of the buffet car. Her mum had given them to her when she'd set off for Spain and she'd totally forgotten about them. Thinking about her mum made her stomach twist a little and just for a second she let herself imagine that her mum was with her. Anna would insist on a high protein snack to keep Kassia's strength up, but Kassia was more in the market for a bag of sweets and some chocolate. She scanned the price-list tacked to the door at the entrance to the buffet car, and began to calculate how much she would be likely to get in exchange for the notes in her hand.

The door slid open. It worked on a sensor and had registered her presence.

There was a rush of warmer air and the sound of chatter; a muddled and indistinct combination of languages that she guessed came from all corners of Europe and beyond.

She looked up from the price-list.

And all the air escaped from her chest as if both her lungs had been punctured.

A man and a teenager were at the counter, offering money to the woman at the cash desk. Neither spoke. Both had their backs to her. One had blond hair and wore a long leather coat, the tails of which fanned out in the air which had been wafted in to the carriage by the opening door.

The door of the couchette pitched open. Jed lurched upright in his bunk, grazing his head on the train ceiling. In the bunk below him, Jacob snorted and spluttered, suddenly ricocheted out of sleep and flung forward for action. Even Dante, who couldn't have heard the noise, but must have been woken by the surge of cold air, gripped tightly to the edge of the shuddering bunk as the door bounced back on its hinges.

Kassia stood on the threshold. Her face was white, her arms outstretched. Money bulged between clenched fingers as if she'd forgotten that she held it.

Jed scrambled down the ladder and steered her

gently inside the carriage, shutting the door firmly behind her.

She seemed to be struggling to find the words she needed. The only sound was the rumbling of the train as it cantered onwards.

'They're here,' she muttered.

Jed couldn't process what he was hearing. 'Who's here?'

Kassia opened her hand and the money fluttered to the floor. With shaking fingers she spelled out four letters.

A deluge of questions flooded Jed's mind. How had NOAH followed them? How did NOAH realise they were on this train? What would NOAH do when they found them?

But only one question escaped from his mouth. 'What do we do now?'

'It's the only way,' said Kassia. She'd no idea if the plan would work but there was no time for indecision. She led Jed, Dante and Jacob along the train corridor and stood now with her hand raised in a fist.

'Let's do this,' urged Jed, encouragingly.

Kassia rapped hard on the couchette door.

There was the sound of movement from inside and then the door cracked open just wide enough for a lanky teenager to peer around it. His wild, bed-head hair edged his face like a broken frame. The shark tooth necklace at the base of his throat glinted and the cuff of bracelets he wore jingled like tiny bells as he held the door ajar.

The boy didn't look surprised to see visitors. In fact, he smiled broadly, ruffled his hand through his hair and then closed one eye into a cheeky wink before pulling the door open more widely. Kassia and the others tumbled inside.

'Come in,' the boy said jokingly, once it was obvious that everyone already had and that the door was now firmly shut behind them.

Kassia looked around apologetically.

With five of them standing between the bunks it was incredibly crowded. The couchette was the same size as the one they'd just left, and Giseppi was obviously not travelling alone. Kassia felt a sudden wave of awkwardness but tried to dismiss this as nerves.

On the top bunk, a girl with long straw-coloured hair was staring down at them. Her face was a puzzle of freckles, her nose wrinkled in confusion. Giseppi nodded up at her. 'Travellers also, Amelie,' he said, as if this basic introduction would explain why their cabin had been invaded at three o'clock in the morning. The girl shrugged and swung her legs around the bunk so her feet dangled amongst the crowd.

Kassia looked around in hope of somewhere to sit. Her heart was racing and there was suddenly not enough air. But the two bottom bunks were piled high with suitcases, bags and trunks. There was literally no space at all.

Giseppi laughed. 'It is crowded in here,' he said. 'But Amelie and I not mind.'

The girl on the top bunk swung her legs playfully.

'Did you have the trouble sleeping?' Giseppi added.

'I need you to disguise us,' Kassia blurted, ignoring his question. Back in their own couchette, they'd reasoned through the approach a little more carefully but now they were here Kassia had lost all sense of building up to her request.

'Ah, you're in need of the painted smile,' said Giseppi.

'Four painted smiles,' Kassia clarified.

'That's a lot of sadness to do the painting over,' said Giseppi.

Kassia nodded and then took a deep breath. 'I told you there were people who were after me.'

To her side, she was aware that Jed was bristling with tension. But how could they ask strangers for help without trying to explain why they were in trouble?

'The thing is,' Kassia went on, 'they're actually after

all of us. And they're *really* after us now. As in, *on this train!*'

'I see.'

If he did really see what she was saying, Giseppi and his beautiful friend, Amelie, seemed incredibly calm about it all.

'These people mustn't find us,' she insisted. 'They're capable of anything. You have to make it so they would never recognise us. Can you do that?'

Giseppi glanced up at the girl who sat on the bunk above him. She twisted a long strand of hair into a coil around her finger and then released it like a spring. A smile beamed across her face.

Giseppi reached down on to the lower bunk and popped open the nearest suitcase. Kassia drank in the smell of greasepaint.

'I am being ready if you are,' Giseppi said.

*The Phoenix* eased to a standstill at Cologne station, its engine chugging gently.

The overhead address system crackled and hummed for a second, then the voice of the train manager began to speak in a tone he obviously kept light and calm for early morning usage.

Kassia could make no sense of the German he was using, but when the message switched to French she made out a few words and numbers. The manager's use of English to round off the announcement confirmed the time and platform for their connection.

They had less than twenty minutes to get to the next train.

Kassia hoped for the hundredth time that evening that Giseppi knew what he was talking about. If the whole train was really full of revellers off to the Festival of Fools then their chances of being hidden amongst them were good. If not, then they'd just spent the last two hours making themselves into living greasepaint targets. NOAH would have a field-day.

Kassia tried to swallow the air bubbling in the back of her throat. She glanced around the couchette at the transformation of those she travelled with, and if she hadn't been scared for their lives, she might have laughed.

Giseppi had begun on Jacob: a thick, red skull cap that fitted tightly over his head. Bald on top, leaving space for a small yellow bowler-hat, tufts of orange hair sprouted from each side of his grease-painted ears, looking like candyfloss clouds. His face was painted red to merge in with the rubber skull cap. Great white domes arched around his eyes, and his red lips had been ringed with a huge white oval, making the space for his mouth reach the base of his nose and the edge of his chin. From a suitcase stuffed with clothing, Amelie had chosen a quilted chequered suit; long, red kipper tie; a shirt with enormous wide collars; and weird padded white gloves that made his hands look too big. There was an enormous felt flower sewn to his lapel. Jacob had shuffled awkwardly into the outfit, embarrassed perhaps, but definitely determined to be dressed quickly, the jacket of his suit almost tearing as he slipped his arm so quickly inside.

Dante's look was less symmetrical. A huge blue ruff made of layered netting ringed his neck. It fanned out so widely that it connected with the bubbly, blue wig he wore, masking his ears completely so that his hearing aids were totally unseen. His face had been painted entirely white. Amelie had added red lips and a red nose, then across one eye she'd painted a green diamond so that his pupil glinted from the centre. The other eye had been turned into a blue star. Red, arched eyebrows ringed each eye and Kassia thought it made Dante look surprised, which she guessed he was.

Jed looked sad but this was entirely deliberate. Minimalist artwork this time meant his face was totally white except for two black diamonds painted over his eyes. From one eye, Giseppi had painted two long, black tears. On his head, Jed wore a black beret to match the stripe of the black and white jumper he wore under black braces attached to black trousers. His hands were covered in white gloves, but these fitted his fingers snugly like a layer of skin.

Kassia's look was black and white themed too. She'd pulled on a long, white, puffy bodysuit and was fiddling now with the fluffy, black pom-pom buttons that worked down to her waist. A layered, white ruff scratched around her neck. In the window of the train, she could see that her face was totally white like Jed's. One black eyebrow was curled at the end, while the other tapered off without a curl. This uneven look was matched by the uneven fringe on the short, black wig Giseppi had pulled tight over her hair. The underneath of her eyes were smudged with lilac and black and it looked to Kassia as if she was melting. It felt perhaps as if she was.

Once they'd disguised everyone else, Amelie and Giseppi had started work on themselves. He'd gone for a white face with red rings round his eyes and thin black slashes running vertically across them and down towards his smudged red lips. He wore a tall, battered top-hat ringed with steampunk watches and clocks. With his tattered, red and black shirt and torn black waistcoat he looked to Kassia like a clown who'd been dragged through time to join them on their adventure.

Amelie, meanwhile, looked as beautiful as a clown

as she had as a regular person. A huge purple bubble wig with a red felt heart attached to it like a decorative flower worked perfectly with her white-painted face, which had been sprinkled with small red hearts and flashes of glitter. Her eyes looked enormous, ringed with soft blue, and separate black lashes painted in place. Her beauty made Kassia feel awkward again and this made Kassia almost laugh too. How could she feel jealous of a clown? And how did she have time to feel anything except scared about NOAH finding them?

As if sensing her discomfort, Giseppi leant in closer. 'You need to do the relaxing,' he said softly, and his top-hat wobbled slightly.

Kassia was entirely sure that the one thing she wouldn't be able to do was relax.

From outside in the corridor she began to hear the clicking and opening of couchette doors.

The engine of the train shuddered a little as if the miles *The Phoenix* had climbed across Europe were finally catching up with it.

Giseppi smiled and the painted grin on his face wrinkled, the greasepaint around his eyes cracking into teeny lines. 'Ready?' he said.

Kassia wasn't sure they were. But there was no going back now. This was either a genius idea, or suicide.

The door to the couchette opened and the train was filled with noise.

Kassia held her breath. She peered outside the carriage.

Would there really be other clowns? Would the disguises work? Would NOAH see through the paint and the wigs? Was it all going to end here after everything they'd been through?

But Giseppi was right.

The corridor was filled with clowns. Tall ones; fat ones; clowns in spotted suits and clowns with huge plastic flowers pinned to their lapels who carried striped umbrellas in their hands, and poles topped with spinning plates tucked under their arms.

The clowns poured out of the train like a multi-coloured tidal wave, spilling around on the platform and surging, as one, towards the platform for the connecting train to Paris.

Kassia clutched tightly to the handle of the battered suitcase Giseppi had given her to carry, and just as the train engine of *The Phoenix* shuddered again and finally grew silent, she stepped out of the carriage and joined the camouflaging throng.

Victor had never seen Cole look so angry. 'What is this?' the older man hissed through clenched teeth, as he battled his way down the corridor of the train bound for Paris.

Victor struggled to know how best to answer.

They'd eaten a little and then slept on the train journey aboard *The Phoenix* from Prague. And it was all supposed to be easier on this regular train, with seats, not couchettes or sleeper compartments where people could hide. They were sure it would be simple to find this boy and his friends.

That was until they'd seen the clowns!

Red faces; green faces; blue hair; orange eyes. Hands in padded gloves; suits too large; shoes enormous. They'd entered an alternative universe where it was impossible to tell whether someone was male or female, old or young, let alone find anyone you needed to find.

'Where are they all going? What's this all for!' Cole hissed again as he strode through the carriage, looking from left to right, his frustration increasing with every glance.

Victor was struggling to keep up. The train was lurching as it sped across France. And the colours and the smell of paint were making him nauseous.

They'd moved through each carriage at least three times since leaving Germany. But they were still no closer to finding their prey.

'Talking hands!' Cole snarled back across his shoulder. 'How hard can it be to find talking hands?'

But Victor knew the answer. There had been one carriage near the front where he'd been hopeful. A silent carriage. Cole had stopped walking. And they'd waited.

A white-faced clown, wearing a top-hat decked with watches, had pulled a stream of coloured handkerchiefs from the inside of his tattered waistcoat. The multi-coloured line had stretched on and on and the clowns seated with him had watched and watched. No one had spoken. But then another clown, dressed all in black and white had stood up and began to mime. Victor had watched the painted black tears wrinkle on his white face. White gloved hands had flicked backwards and forwards. There had been silent laughter. A girl with glittered hearts painted on her cheeks had grinned encouragingly. But was this sign language? Was this dance? Were they talking or acting? None of the normal rules applied. Everything here was mixed up.

Cole strode on through the carriage and Victor hurried after him.

There was a clown leaning by the window. Perhaps waiting to move on down to the buffet car. Cole looked him up and down. A yellow face. Green wig.

le 96 Decembre 1999

UNE TRANCHE D'AMOUR

CAKE PARIS
9-11
RUE DU JOUR
PARIS

: ANDREE-LISE
: 000327

GIEUSE                          €2.50
N AU CHOCOLAT                    €2.00

+%                    TAX:        €0.00

TAL:       €4.50

Victor watched as Cole reached out and tightened his hand on the lapel of the clown's suit.

The yellow face wrinkled. Cracks in the paint. Eyes under green eyebrows narrowed. A gloved hand pushed down into a suit pocket.

And then Cole recoiled, a misting of water splashing in his face from the plastic flower sewn to the clown's lapel.

Victor steered Cole away and down the corridor. 'It wasn't him, mate. We just have to keep looking.'

But Victor knew that even if Fulcanelli was on the train, he was submerged. Not in river water this time. But in fabric and wigs and greasepaint. And their chances of finding him were slipping away like water rushing towards the sea.

'You need to calm down,' Jed whispered.

Kassia was shaking again. The uneven fringe of her wig and the non-matching eyebrows made her look totally unbalanced. The black and lilac smudging below her eyes shimmered like tears and her stiff paper ruff was crinkled awkwardly, creased more severely at one side of her neck than the other.

'They didn't see us,' Jed said again. He wanted to take her hand and squeeze it. To try and force her to believe it was going to be all right, but his hand swung nervously at his side.

He could tell she was barely able to focus. 'They were so close,' she spluttered. 'And when you stood up, I was so scared.'

It was obvious she could hardly bring herself to think back on the encounter. The mime had been a risk. But Victor and Cole had fallen for it and so now everyone just needed to keep their heads or all their efforts to go unnoticed would be wasted.

Jed flexed his fingers so that his gloved hand brushed against Kassia's, their little fingers linking for just the time it took him to breathe. A tiny smile flickered across her unpainted pink lips, bright now against the white of her skin.

Outside the window of the train, it was fully light. The buildings denser. The centre of Paris drawing closer.

'We have to do this, Kassia. Everything we've done so far has been about getting the recipe. And we have to keep our cover. Understand?'

She nodded and the uneven wig shifted a fraction on her head.

So Giseppi talked them through the plan. He seemed more serious now he'd seen Victor and Cole up close. The black slashes across his eyes, beneath the ticking clocks on his battered top-hat, looked sinister in the brightness of midday and Jed wondered, not for the first time, how it was that they had put all their trust in a man and a girl they'd met only hours before. Surely their experience with Andel should have taught them to be more careful. But the choices had been limited. Trust the clowns to disguise them. Or jump from another moving train.

Now they were in too deep, fully immersed in a sea of playacting and pretence.

Jed shook himself and nodded at Giseppi who was still talking, his accent softly lilting in a reassuring way. He'd asked if the plan made sense. Jed wasn't totally sure, but at the moment he was only sure of one thing. The recipe they needed was in the cathedral. And the cathedral was only minutes away.

The mass of clowns and painted people moved as one from the train to the subway. Even if Jed and the others had wanted to choose an alternative route, their chances of breaking free of the crowds were minimal. They progressed like a stream of animals boarding an ark as travellers poured from the platform at Gare du Nord station. And more clowns joined them, from buses and from the streets. All surging towards the metro train that would take them in the direction of Saint-Michel.

The train, when it stopped at the platform, was

already full. More clowns, carrying silk flowers and jesters' sticks topped with three-horned bells, drove forward and crammed inside. Giseppi took the lead and pushed amongst the crowds as the doors slid open.

'I'm right with you,' Jed reassured, as Kassia clambered on to the train, the case she carried banging against Jacob and Dante's legs as they squeezed up to make room for her. The doors made a hissing noise like a snake.

Kassia looked back, her eyes frantic. 'Quick, Jed!'

He stumbled into the carriage as the doors hissed again and slid closed behind him. As he turned, the hand of a passenger still stranded on the platform banged hard on the window. It stayed there for a moment, fingers splayed, palm sweaty.

From inside the train, Jed's eyes locked on Victor's. It was his hand pressed tight to the glass.

For a second, confusion swam in Victor's eyes.

Jed remembered the look from hours ago. On the train down from the Petřín tower. When Jed had twisted the intercom cable around Victor's neck, squeezing tighter and tighter before he finally released him. The confusion was the same. But then suddenly there was another look.

Recognition. He'd seen through Jed's disguise.

Victor's hand slid from the window as the train

pulled away from the platform. In the misting on the glass, it was possible to see the life-line marks across the imprint of Victor's palm. They ran from the top to the bottom, as if his life would stretch on forever. But the marks on his palm were a lie. There were things that needed to be done, if you wanted to live forever.

Jed's heart thundered inside him as the train roared through the underground.

'You OK?' Kassia said urgently.

She hadn't seen Victor through the crowd. She hadn't seen the palm print. And so Jed said nothing.

As they approached Saint-Michel station, Giseppi gestured towards the door. The train slowed, and there could be no doubt they'd reached their destination. The carriage emptied as the clowns travelled en masse past the buskers and up on to street level.

The air was cold, a surprise to the system, and Jed drank it in.

The noise of the city was almost overwhelming as they marched in step with the crowds, turning left and spilling along the pavement. It was difficult to walk quickly. Street vendors worked from behind stalls with green awnings, selling paintings and postcards of the city. Trestle tables were stocked with small metal statues of the Eiffel Tower. They reminded Jed of Petřín and he felt anger knot inside his stomach.

He tried to tell himself that none of that mattered now. They were where they needed to be. And he tried not to look over his shoulder to see if they were still being followed.

Jed almost expected to see the dragon, swirling and twisting, filling his mind with memories. But the reality of now was too sharp and too intense.

Until they crossed the road, and walked across a small bridge that stretched across the River Seine.

A dragon began to spin and spin in front of Jed's eyes so that he could see nothing except the building that it framed.

Notre Dame Cathedral.

The building filled his vision, both in reality and in memory. The sounds and smells of the city and the river and of the moment were so piercing, Jed could hardly stand. Kassia was watching him and he was aware that the painted tears on his cheek were more honest than his attempt to smile at her.

They were here. The answer was here. And soon all the fighting and the running and the fear would be over.

The cathedral was huge. The lines of the walls straight and regular, the two towers tall and castle-like. There was no sweeping dome like St Paul's. Everything about Notre Dame was sharp.

Below the two turreted towers was a long arcade of points that looked to Jed like jagged teeth. Below that, in the centre, was a huge rose window. This was protected by skinnier windows that stuck out on niches made of the same sandy stone as the rest of the building. Below the rose window were three enormous arches. Each was made of layered stone and sat around the edge of one of three massive doorways. There were life-size figures carved into the stone, which stood like guards to the entrance, but the decoration was so overwhelming and intricate that it was impossible to work out who the figures were.

The space in front of the cathedral was paved like a courtyard. It was crammed with clowns for the festival. There were stilt-walkers; jugglers; and a man dressed completely in flowing, purple satin who seemed to be trying to paint the sky with fire. There were unicyclists; musicians; and fortune-tellers with painted faces and peacock feathers in their hair.

Around the edge of the square, vendors were selling popcorn from tall glass containers attached to wagons with huge, golden wheels. From a battered blue cart, a man scooped pralines, roasted in sugar, into long paper cones, and beside him, a woman whipped candyfloss into wide, pink circles. There was a crêpe seller cooking thin crispy pancakes on a thick metal pan above a flaming griddle. And in the far corner, to the left of the cathedral, beside a statue of a rider on a horse, a plump man in a long striped apron served shellfish and crab from a towering arrangement of bowls and containers balanced precariously on mounds of steaming crushed ice. The air prickled with the smell of sugar and salt and the sea.

'So, the Festival of Fools,' Giseppi said, widening his arms as if he individually had brought the celebration to the centre of Paris.

'Thank you for getting us here. And for keeping us safe,' Kassia said.

Giseppi grinned, and his face creased so much that the dark painted slashes across his eyes disappeared within folds of skin. The hands on one of the watches pinned to his top-hat were spinning wildly. 'Any time,' he said. 'If you ever are in the need of a painted smile, or the help of any sort at all,' he added, 'then I'm your man.'

Jed watched Kassia grin, and he was sure that under the face paint she wore, she was blushing. He felt an emotion he wasn't sure he'd felt before and he shook himself to try and make it go away. Giseppi was still talking.

'Besides, you have now the time to celebrate with us, haven't you? Now you have done the getting away from those guys who were doing the chasing?'

Jed didn't answer.

'Dump your stuff here.' Giseppi pointed to a cart filled with cases and bags that had been left by other clowns. They were propped in position next to a nest of long sticks which Jed guessed were for use with the heap of diabolos beside them. Jacob took Dante's bag and stacked it with the other cases and trunks the revellers had brought with them from the train. 'You should now enjoy the carnival,' Giseppi went on. 'You've done what you wanted after all. The getting away, I mean.'

But that wasn't *all* that they wanted. There were things Giseppi didn't know.

If Jed was right, then the recipe for the elixir was almost within touching distance. And as much as he knew that the others would have enjoyed the chance to relax, Jed understood that was not an option.

Even if the others hadn't seen for themselves, Victor and Cole had followed them and the chase wasn't over.

Kassia could see that Jed was trembling. A stilt-walker was manoeuvring among the crowds, juggling knives as he walked. Kassia thought they'd taken enough risks for a while and moved Jed well out of his way.

Jed's hand was shaking and tiny beads of sweat were lining the edge of his painted mask. The blackened tears had begun to run.

She decided it was ridiculous to ask if he was OK. If what he'd worked out in Prague was true, then they were moments away from finding answers. But every moment took them closer to an edge she couldn't bear to imagine crossing if they'd got things wrong. And she could see his body was fighting. She reached up nervously and wiped a line of sweat from above his eyes. It left a smudge of white across the tips of her fingers.

Jed looked down to the ground.

'Are you telling me everything?' she asked gently.

The crowds were cheering the stilt-walker. The blades of the knives were cartwheeling in the dying sun of the evening. 'Of course.'

This time she knew he was lying. His face, masked with greasepaint, was almost unreadable, but his eyes had the same look they'd had in the hospital in Heidelberg. That was the day he'd tried to keep from her what he'd worked out about the six doses of the elixir.

'Jed? What is it?'

'Victor saw me,' he said quietly.

'On the train. I know. With the miming and the

signs. And I was so scared that he'd work it out.'

'He *did* work it out. Not then. But on the metro.'

'Victor was on the metro?'

Jed nodded.

'But there were hundreds of people. Everyone dressed up.'

'He recognised me, Kass.'

She bit the edge of her lip. 'So what does that mean?'

'That we have to be quick. We have to get into the cathedral and we have to find that book, then get out.'

She'd wanted to wait. A chance just to be safe. But there was not enough time, never enough. They had to keep going. She rubbed her hands, and the greasepaint from Jed's face soaked into her skin. 'So that's what we do,' she said. 'We keep going.'

He looked for a second across at the Seine and Kassia followed his gaze. She reasoned it was possible to believe the river wasn't there. It was almost hidden as it circled round the island that supported the cathedral. But the river was *always* there. Gushing onwards. Never standing still.

Jed looked at her as if he knew she understood. 'Maybe this is the time that things will work out for us, at the side of a river, don't you think?'

She felt her heart racing. 'We can always hope that,' she said.

'OK.' He took a deep breath and moved back with her towards where Jacob and Dante were standing transfixed beneath the spinning knives. 'We ready to do this thing?'

'Seriously? You want us to look *now*?' signed Dante. 'Have you seen the crêpe stall? Can't we just have some time to chill?'

Kassia watched Jed run every possible answer and justification through his head. But the sign he chose in reply was simple. 'No.' Then he led the way through the crowd towards the entrance to Notre Dame.

The noise levels rose so that it was impossible to distinguish one sound from another. A minstrel playing a mandolin jigged across their path. A street vendor wearing a tray of popcorn scooped servings into red and white chequered bags, calling out the prices in time with an accordionist who was standing on an upturned crate, beating a drum with a stick attached to a foot pedal. A circle of clowns swirled forwards and backwards in time with the music and the chanting, as if they were dancing some speeded up version of the Hokey Cokey. But Jed ignored all of it as he strode towards the cathedral doors.

Once inside, the noise of the Festival evaporated.

It was good there was nothing to hear because there was so much to see that it was overwhelming. The nave of the cathedral stretched down towards the altar and up to a roof that looked like a circus-tent canopy made entirely of stone. Back in London, the ceiling of St Paul's had been decorated with pictures and paintings. The ceiling of Notre Dame was bare. But beautiful. The stone looked warm, glowing almost, in the light of prayer candles that had been lit along row after row, down the side of the cathedral. The light from the flames bounced from the enormous rose window, soaking the building in a rainbow of spilt light.

The urgency of the chase faded away. Kassia forgot that they were racing the clock, that they needed to find the recipe or Jed would die. The beauty took her breath away. She knew Jed saw it too, and for a second he had allowed himself to forget.

But the moment died.

'Why are you so totally sure that it will be here?' Dante said with his hands.

They hadn't talked about it. Jed had seemed so certain and they'd trusted him to know.

Jed flexed his gloved fingers as if trying to latch on to the signs he needed for it all to make sense to the others. 'Paris. It's where I found the elixir. And the title of the first book I wrote and even the second.

*Cathedrals; Dwelling places.* When I came out of the Thames in London I knew I had to go to St Paul's. But it was the wrong cathedral.' He looked across at Kassia. 'Not wrong because of what happened after.' He bit his lip. 'I mean, wrong for the elixir. Being here, a cathedral in Paris, well that just *fits*.' He took a deep breath. 'This place feels like home somehow. As if I might have spent hours here thinking about . . . well, you know.'

'Playing God?' Kassia said quietly. She remembered their discussion in the woods by the Devil's Stone.

'Too heavy for me, mate,' said Dante, making his signs light. 'Not sure what I believe about the whole creator thing.'

'But look at what the people who built this cathedral thought,' said Jed widening his hands. 'Look at this stone story about a higher power. It doesn't matter what we think or believe. This place is where huge ideas are written for people to see. And I think, if I was in Paris when I made the elixir, then this is the place where I would have asked Canseliet to store the recipe. It feels right.'

'It's pretty big,' Jacob whispered. 'Lots of potential places to hide things. Where do we start?'

They walked down the nave. Dante was leading this time, steering them towards the left of the cathedral.

'Any flashbacks? Any memories?' asked Kassia.

Jed's face was pinched. 'I can't tell. It feels familiar. It feels right. But . . .'

'It's OK. We're trying to find where *Canseliet* hid the book. Not Fulcanelli. You don't have to remember.'

He smiled in gratitude.

Dante stopped walking. He pointed to a large sign stretched across the side of the inner wall, then he spelled each letter out with his fingers. '*Trésor de Notre Dame*. The Treasury. What d'you think?'

Kassia scanned the sign. Her heart flipped. 'It says they keep all sorts of valuables here. Part of the true cross of Jesus; a nail from his crucifixion, even his crown of thorns.'

'So if you were going to hide the recipe for an elixir that could make you live for ever, then maybe you'd hide it near to all these other precious things,' urged Jacob, his painted, white grin widening. 'Security on this part of the cathedral must be tight. It would make a pretty safe hiding place, that's for sure.'

Jed nodded. 'Greatest treasure in the world, NOAH said to me before I knew what they were on about. It would make sense if it was hidden here.'

The Treasury of Notre Dame was set out like a small museum. Glass display cases housed statues made of silver and crosses made of brass, encrusted

226

with spectacular jewels. There were golden chalices; wall hangings and tiny paintings in elaborate gilded frames. They scanned the treasures, pressing their hands against the glass that kept the prizes out of reach.

But where was the ultimate prize? The reason they'd travelled so far? Obviously it wouldn't be out on public display, but maybe there was a clue here about where Canseliet had chosen for safe keeping; a sign or a symbol that would make things clear.

They investigated every cabinet; scanned every exhibition board; searched every shelf.

In the very last presentation case, Kassia found what she thought must be the crown of thorns. An extravagant, decorated container had been made to house the twisted wooden circle. Through the glass ring that clothed it, held up by silver angels and golden cherubs, it was impossible, though, to see the crown itself.

And it was impossible to believe they'd searched every part of the Treasury.

Jed stood beside her. He was so close, their shoulders almost touched.

Kassia took a moment before she said anything. She didn't want him to move away. 'You don't think the book is here?' she asked nervously.

'It's *not* here,' he said, and he pulled his arms across his chest so that their shoulders slipped further apart.

'But it's not going to be out on show, is it? Maybe we've just missed a sign. Maybe . . .' She didn't know what she was going to say. She just couldn't bear to think they'd come this far and failed.

'The book's not here, Kassia. A crown of thorns; a crucifixion nail; a piece of the cross. Some of the most important treasures in history. But the book with the recipe for eternal life? I think I'd know if we were close. There'd be some connection, some memory, something. But there's nothing here.'

And any chance at all she had of offering a sensible answer, died in her mouth.


'So what do we do now?' The four of them were seated on a line of pews hidden at the corner of the cathedral, just behind the Treasury. It was quiet. Some revellers from the Festival dipped in and out of the cathedral, some lighting candles and some stopping for a while, to sit and bow their heads in meditation.

It seemed almost normal now to see those in costume mingling with tourists in plain clothes. What was not normal was the panic surging in Kassia's stomach. In Prague they'd followed the clues and the symbols and even when escaping from the Petřín

Tower they had been moving forward. And the time in the tunnels had seemed so full of hope. And now . . . nothing. If Canseliet really had hidden Fulcanelli's book in an attempt to keep it safe, then it wasn't with all the treasures inside the vast stone book of Notre Dame Cathedral. The trail had run cold.

Kassia looked at Jed. He'd been so sure, and now he looked empty. Broken even. He was sitting with his head lowered into his hands. To those who walked by, he probably looked as if he was praying. Kassia feared that what he was really doing was crying. Not pretend tears this time, painted on to his face as decoration. But real tears. Because the search was over. She wanted to reach out and say something, anything, that would make it better. But there was nothing she could say.

It had grown dark outside. The beauty of the rose window had faded and the light in the cathedral had morphed from multi-coloured to just the amber glow of the candles.

Kassia shook herself. This was ridiculous! It couldn't be over! Were they really just going to sit here until evening turned into night and accept that all their efforts were for nothing? Were they really giving up so easily?

She stood up and as she did so, a little boy dressed as a jester dashed in front of her. She staggered backwards, her legs hitting the pew behind her. The little boy hesitated. His face broke into a toothy grin. 'Pardon, mademoiselle,' he said, reaching to steady the plastic golden crown he wore.

'That's OK,' Kassia mumbled.

A woman moved forward and grabbed his hand. 'I'm sorry,' she said, registering Kassia's use of English. 'Pascal is very excited. He's just been crowned prince as part of the Festival of Fools. He wants everyone to see his crown.'

Kassia nodded and smiled at the little boy who tapped the edge of the plastic headgear again, just in case she hadn't fully appreciated its beauty. And as she nodded and focused on the crown, a collection of thoughts knotted together, like brambles intertwining round her head.

'I remember,' she said urgently, as the mother led the little Prince of Fools away.

'You remember where Canseliet hid the book?' gasped Jacob.

'No. But I remember about the Festival of Fools and why I knew about it.' As soon as Giseppi had mentioned it on the train, she'd known she'd heard of it before, but she just couldn't place its importance. 'Victor Hugo's *Hunchback of Notre Dame*, remember?'

'Nope, never read it,' signed Dante.

'Well Mum forced me to. The Festival of Fools: it's in the book. And everything is topsy-turvy, just like today.'

'Topsy-turvy?'

'The wrong way round. Fools crowned as kings. Little boys made into monarchs. That sort of thing.'

'Are you going somewhere with this?' pressed Dante, as Jed lifted his head so as not to miss the signed answers to Kassia's increasingly frantic discussion.

'That's important. So hold that thought.'

'There's more then?'

Kassia ploughed on. 'In the book there's this guy called Frollo. He's a sort of priest here, I think, but he has a secret. He's into alchemy.'

Jed was concentrating fully now.

'And that's not his only secret, either. Quasimodo.' She said the word with such vigour she made it sound like the thought was exploding out of her. 'He was this abandoned baby and Frollo took him in and sort of looked after him. And he kept him hidden in the cathedral. But it's the hidden bit that's important. And the alchemy. And the secret.'

'You're losing me, sis. Can't you make things a little clearer?'

Kassia took a deep breath. 'Frollo kept Quasimodo secret in the bell tower. Topsy-turvy you see. Not

231

down here in the Treasury. But up high with the bells.'

'And the fool as king thing? How does that fit in?'

Jed was focused totally now as Kassia moved her hands to answer. 'The fool becomes a king. The reverse of what's expected. The recipe won't be hidden in a treasury. I think Canseliet would have hidden Fulcanelli's book where Frollo the alchemist hid what was important to him. I think it will be in the bell tower.'

'There are two bell towers,' said Jacob. 'How do we know which one?'

Kassia thought back to when they'd stood with the other clowns on the courtyard outside the cathedral. She remembered the towers either side of the building, like turrets on a castle. The bells must be spread across both towers.

'So we split up,' suggested Jacob. 'Two of us take each tower.'

Kassia felt a wave of panic. She didn't want to split up. But it seemed childish to argue. 'OK. I'll go with Jed to one and you and Dante take the other.'

'I should go with Jed.' Jacob's voice was determined and he didn't even bother turning his words into signs. It seemed odd to see someone whose face was still red and wearing a huge whitened grin look so serious beneath the greasepaint.

Kassia stared across at Jed. She didn't want to be separate from him.

'He might need me,' went on Jacob.

Kassia's answer was muffled and under her breath. 'What if he needs *me*?'

'We're going to be climbing high,' said Jacob 'And we can't risk what happened on the O2.'

How could Jacob use that as an argument? He hadn't even been there. It was Kassia who'd helped get Jed safely down to the ground. 'The stuff on the O2 was because your memory was coming back,' Kassia said, looking towards Jed to try and include him.

'And you don't think this climb will involve memory return?' pressed Jacob. 'Think about it. We're in the city Fulcanelli lived in. Worked in. Found the answers in. And if the book he wrote is really in the bell tower, then we have no idea how that's going to affect Jed's memory. I should be there. Keep him safe.'

Kassia glanced across at Jed again. Did he want this? Did he think Jacob was a better support than her?

Dante stepped forward and stretched his signs so all of them could see. 'We could always do both towers together. Who knows? We might only need to search one anyway.'

'No.' Jed's answer was emphatic.

'OK, mate. I was just saying.'

'We don't have time.'

Kassia took a deep breath. Jed was right. If Victor and Cole had made it to the cathedral then there was no time to waste choosing teams. They were one team, trying to travel in two directions. Splitting up made sense.

'You and Jed take the South Tower and Dante and I will take the North,' Kassia signed. She didn't speak her answer. She was afraid that for the moment her voice would be too shaky.

She reached out a hand. An attempt to touch Jed on the shoulder, to show her encouragement. But Jed had already moved away. He and Jacob were heading for the exit.

Once they were back outside, the noise again was overpowering. The sound of dancers and singers seemed amplified. It was dark now but the Festival organisers had lit flaming torches along the edge of the courtyard and the flames dipped and danced against the black of a night sky. The gaggle of clowns looked even more other-worldly now and Jed had to remind himself that he looked as if he was one of them. Not an outsider, but one who belonged.

Jacob led Jed towards the side of the cathedral and up a tiny flight of stairs. This was obviously the entrance to the bell tower. A sign in French had some information about the enormous bell housed inside and there were photographs laminated to the sign. Jed scanned the information. Seemed the bell even had a name. Emmanuel.

This was all great. But the door to the tower was shut: when Jacob tried the handle, it didn't open.

'So what do we do?' asked Jed.

Jacob's yellow bowler-hat was slipping awkwardly to one side, kept in place only by the tufts of orange hair. And the white edging of his painted grin was so smudged that red from his cheeks was bleeding into the line. He glanced over his shoulder. The party was picking up and all the main action was in the front of the cathedral. No one was looking their way.

Jacob gave one more glance to his left. Then he rolled up the sleeves of his baggy chequered suit and his tattoos rippled on his arms.

'What are you doing?' Jed winced.

Jacob shoulder-barged hard against the door.

Jed tried to swallow his surprise. 'This is a cathedral, *remember*!'

'And we're racing the clock, *remember*! We don't have time to wait around. I'm thinking that notice says something along the lines of how no one can go up and see the bells outside certain hours. Do you want *that* to be your answer, Jed? That your time's run out?'

'No! I just . . .'

'Just what? Want to play by the rules? I think we've been patient long enough, don't you?'

Jed felt strangely uncomfortable. Sure, they'd hidden in the underground tunnels in Prague when they shouldn't have. But breaking and entering . . . in a cathedral? Jacob seemed totally sure about this, though.

'I'm not always an angel,' said Jacob, and his smudged artificial grin twisted in a way that made him look more than a little sinister.

The door had opened out on to a stone staircase. It looked like the stairs corkscrewed upwards but it was impossible to tell how far, because the space was unlit. Jed ran his hand up and down the stonework, feeling for a light switch. Nothing. Weird. Maybe the staircase was only used in the daylight. Or maybe the lighting was controlled somewhere centrally inside Notre Dame.

Jacob moved back across the threshold. 'More than one way to find light,' he said, and grabbed two large, flaming torches from the attachments that ringed the side of the square.

Jed took one and watched the flame flicker. 'Seriously?'

'You have a better idea?'

Jed didn't.

The staircase curled into the tower and Jed used the metal handrail driven on to the stone to keep himself steady. Every now and then there was a window set in the curve of the wall. But the sky was so dark that it offered no extra light at all. They used the torches to guide them and kept on climbing. The flames cast ghostly shadows, which stretched and twisted as they walked. The only sound was the fall of their feet on the stone treads as they moved higher. And their breathing. Jed could hear the air catching in Jacob's throat.

Eventually, the staircase opened up. They'd reached some sort of gallery or display space. The ceiling was high above them and down the sides of the walls ran a long window. Tiny pieces of glass jigsawed together to make one enormous segmented sheet. The light from the torches bounced against the fragments and fractured across the walls. Jed felt weirdly disorientated. But it was clear this was not the section of the tower that housed the bell.

In the corner, display boards showed pictures from Victor Hugo's book. Jed scanned the images. This was the right tower though, he *knew* it. The signs showed this space was where Quasimodo brought Esmeralda in the story of the Hunchback of Notre Dame. So this tower surely had to be the one Canseliet chose to keep Fulcanelli's book safe.

They found more stairs curling upwards and this time Jacob's breathing was louder, as if he was struggling to keep going. Jed looked down at his feet, watching carefully for the lip of each step.

Suddenly, on the outside edge of the stairwell, there was an opening. A square arch led out on to some sort of balcony that looked as if it ran along the outside of the tower. A door had been wedged open by a long wooden prop, jammed in the door hinge. Noise from the traffic joined with the noise of the Festival and flooded in through the opening. Jed waited a moment to catch his breath as drums beat in the square below and the crowds cheered.

'Nearly there,' encouraged Jacob, his chest rising and falling, so the red kipper tie lifted up and down against the front of his oversized suit.

Jed turned away from the opening and continued to make his way up into the tower.

The stairs climbed onwards and then suddenly the surface below Jed's feet changed. Wood, not stone. He could feel air blowing in between the open slat work, a sign of the space falling away below them to allow the bell to ring.

The space had opened up into what looked like a loft in an old country barn. In the light of the torches, it was possible to see beams criss-crossing overhead forming a roof and then extending down to make a structure which supported an enormous and impressive bell.

'This is it,' said Jed. 'The great Emmanuel.'

Jacob reached up and took the yellow bowler-hat from his head. His hair line was sweating under the rubber skull cap. The definition of the painting around his eyes was almost impossible to make out now. He rubbed his face with the hand that held the hat, and the paint smudged into an ugly red and grey smear.

They'd reached the bell tower. But there were no fancy glass display cabinets or elaborate cases like the one that had held the crown of thorns downstairs in the Treasury.

They clambered round the loft, spilling the light from the flaming torches across every corner of the space they'd climbed to. Jed reached high and bent down low. He crawled on his stomach into the furthest corners he could reach. He stepped up on the lowest beams of the bell support and flung the light as far as he could, into the recesses above and to the side of him.

But there was nothing. Just an enormous bell, hanging silently from wooden rafters.

And no sign at all of the book they'd been searching for.

'Maybe it's in the other tower?' suggested Jacob, and his voice sounded almost frenzied.

Jed shook his head. Maybe. But this place felt right. Almost familiar.

He held the torch high and the light danced. The flame sparked, and just for a moment, Jed saw his face reflected on the polished surface of the Emmanuel bell.

He said the name again inside his head. He had a feeling he knew what the word meant. Something about God being with us. How would he know that? Unless he was connecting to things Fulcanelli had known. This had to make the bell tower the right place.

He lowered the torch and his hand began to shake. A wave of confusion and doubt seemed to swell up from the wooden floor he stood on and consume him. God being with us. He remembered the connection. But his mind took him back to just before the Devil's Stone and the discussion outside the Treasury. Playing God. Is that really what he'd done? They'd come here to look for the recipe for eternal life, but wasn't that something that only God should be in charge of? If there was a God. He wasn't sure he was clear about that. He wasn't clear about much any more.

But somehow he knew that if Canseliet had hidden the book containing the recipe anywhere in Notre Dame, then it would have been in this tower.

Jed's hand was shaking more violently, so he reached out to steady himself. The metal of the bell was surprisingly cold to the touch.

'You OK, mate?'

Jed wanted to scream. That question again! How could he possibly answer that?

He looked across at Jacob. 'I'm trying to figure it all out and make the connections and there're so many pieces to this puzzle.'

He felt a wave of nausea surging in his stomach. His hand slipped and he was sure he was going to black out. This was madness. The feeling from the O2 all over again. Jacob had said it might happen, but where was the memory? Where was the spinning dragon to show him the answers?

'I need air,' he blurted.

He turned from the giant bell and stumbled down the steps towards the arched opening that led out on to the tower balcony. This narrow walkway was edged with a wide stone wall which came up to waist height. Positioned on the wall were various stone statues and sculptures, looking down on to the city. Metal fencing had been carefully connected from the top of the wall, stretching upwards to above head height, and then across to the side of the tower. It was clearly there to try and prevent people from falling from the balcony. Jed grabbed for the metal fencing in an attempt to stop himself from tripping. He felt like he was inside a cage. He felt less sick but was suddenly afraid.

The sound from the courtyard drifted up to the tower and merged again with the traffic noise from the city. It made the fun of the Festival feel a lifetime away and totally out of reach. He lowered his forehead against the metal grating and looked out across the buildings that networked away from the great cathedral.

The sky seemed lighter than before. Clouds had cleared and the moon was visible now, a pale, white globe in a starless sky. Traces of cloud still straggled across the surface, making it look like the moon was made of water. As Jed peered through the bars, he could just make out the outline of the River Seine carving its way through Paris.

'I think the book's in this tower,' said Jed. 'But I don't know why. And I don't know where.'

Jacob was standing to his left, his back against the wall.

Jed was aware of the line of stone gargoyles and grotesques to the side of Jacob. He had some vague understanding of the difference between these weird stone creatures. If they carried rain water away from the building, through water spouts in their mouths, they were gargoyles. But some other stone figures of beasts and monsters seemed to serve no purpose at all except for decoration. These were called grotesques. And that's what they were: truly ugly and monstrous. Jed pulled away from the grating. One stone beast was clearer to see than the others. It was a huge demon, sitting hunched on the wall of the balcony. His wings were folded in behind him, and from this angle it looked as if Jacob's and the demon's body were joined. That Jacob had become part of the stone story of the cathedral.

Suddenly, ideas began to shuffle in Jed's mind. 'Stone books,' he blurted. 'We knew the recipe had something to do with stone books. And that's why we went to Prague. And then we thought this place was a stone book in itself. Remember?'

Jacob's painted face was narrowed in concentration, the sculpted wings of the demon framing his body as if they belonged to him.

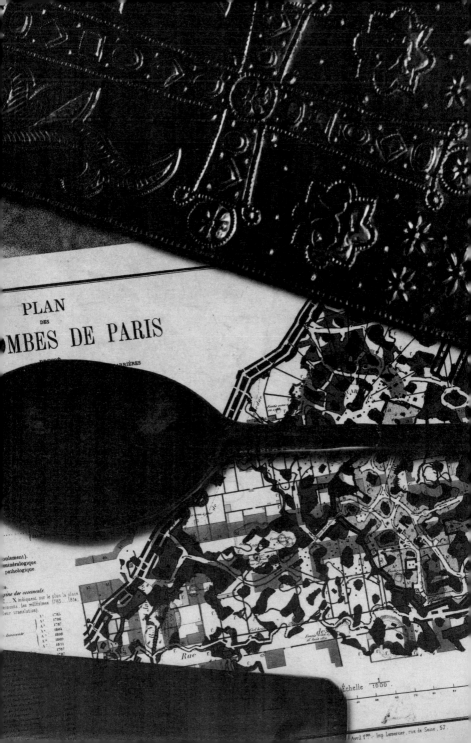

PLAN

DES

MBES DE PARIS

RRIÈRES

oulement).
minéralogique
pathologique

gine des cevements.
X indiquent sur le plan la place
ments. les millésimes 1785...1834,
leur translation)

A.° 1785.
A.° 1786.
A.° 1787.
A.° 1804.
A.° 1808.
A.° 1800.
A.° 1811.
A.° 1787.

Rue

Échelle ⸺ 1000.

Avril fʳᵉ ⸺ Imp Lemercier, rue de Seine, 57.

'What if that's the key?' Jed pressed on. 'The stone bit and the story that the cathedral's telling? What if Canseliet *did* hide the recipe here in this tower, but inside the stone of the cathedral's story?'

'Amongst these gargoyles and grotesques, then?' asked Jacob.

'Exactly. To protect its story. It makes sense, doesn't it?' Jed could hear the hope mounting in his own voice. He began to walk along the balcony, holding the flaming torch high and spilling its light across the stone characters that guarded the tower.

As he walked, the light swam away from the demon and spilled on to the back of a huge stone bird. An eagle, perhaps. Jed put his hand on to the stone wings and a bolt of memory surged through him. Behind his eyes, a dragon turned and turned and in the centre of the vision, Jed saw a group of men huddled round a roaring fire. The memory was so real, Jed almost believed he could slip into the frame and join them. But the memory felt different to the memories the dragon had framed for him before. There was no pain attached, only an overwhelming feeling of happiness and hope and expectation. It was the same feeling he'd had in the underground alchemical laboratory in Prague. In the light of the newly revealed moon, Jed suddenly felt excitement and not fear.

Was the image he saw one of him working with his friends to find the elixir? Was the memory from when hope had been so close? He pressed his hand against the eagle. But the image was fragmenting, slipping away like water, running from the mouth of a gargoyle down the roof of Notre Dame to join the waters of the Seine.

Everything inside him told him that the book they searched for had to be in reach.

He walked around the edge of the balcony and on the corner, bathed by the moonlight, was another grotesque. A dragon.

Jed put his hand on the scaly back of the dragon and his fingers burned. He saw the dragon in his mind again, spinning and spinning; the stone dragon from the balcony standing inside the frame of the memory as if it was alive. For a moment, Jed really believed the beast would rise up and break free of the stone, stretch his wings and fly.

'It's close,' Jed yelled. 'Really close! I *know* it!'

He ran his hands down the stone dragon and clutched at the wall. He dragged his hand along the brickwork. And then his fingers stopped.

Crudely carved on to the bricks below the stone dragon was a faint and tiny design. A triangle. Inside the triangle was a square and inside this, a circle. Jed could hardly breathe. He pushed his palm flat against the symbol. Suddenly, the dragon in his mind spun again and this time the memory was loud and painful. Tyres squealing; a car racing out of control; a man's face behind a windscreen; eyes wide; mouth open in scream; a medallion glinting at the base of his throat.

Jed closed his eyes. The memory burned and scored behind his eyes. Then it darkened and drifted away, leaving only the image of the medallion. A triangle, around a square, around a circle.

Jed knew this sign. And more importantly, he remembered now what it meant. 'The Philosopher's Stone!' he blurted. 'Why didn't we work that out earlier?'

Jacob was kneeling next to him, his too-baggy suit creased around his shoulders, his yellow bowler-hat discarded beside him on the ground.

'The book of stone. The Philosopher's Stone. That's what the recipe needed all along. It's the centre of the recipe. The thing alchemists need before they can even begin to think about making the elixir. All our research on alchemy went on and on about the Philosopher's Stone. *Our* book of stone was connected to the Philosopher's Stone. Part of the stone story here at Notre Dame.'

Jacob's face showed only confusion. 'I don't get

how this helps us.'

Jed spread his hand across the etched symbol on the brick. 'I think it's here.'

'You're not making sense, mate. What's here? The Philosopher's Stone?'

'No. The recipe for the elixir, hidden under the mark of the Philosopher's Stone. A symbol to lead us to what we would need.' Jed pushed his hand hard against the brick. It wobbled for a moment, the plaster keeping it in place, falling like a dusting of tears. Jed held the torch high so he could see more clearly. Then he dug his nails into the flaking plaster line above the brick and carefully eased it free.

Once the brick had been removed from the wall, Jed shone the torch into the opening.

Lying in the dust and the plaster was a small, brown, oilskin bundle. Jed reached inside and pulled it out. He passed the torch to Jacob and held the bundle between both his hands.

Very carefully, he began to undo the oilskin wrapping.

And when the skin had fallen fully free, in the light of the moon and the two torches Jacob held, Jed could see clearly what he'd found.

The manuscript was bound in leather. Jed pressed one finger against the image scored across it. A dragon, curled in a circle and eating its tail. The ouroboros. Image of eternal life.

A wave of happiness flooded from his fingers up into his chest as if he'd taken the heat from the flaming torch and poured it inside himself.

From beside him, Jacob's voice was just a whisper. 'Is it in there? The recipe?'

Jed flicked open the pages. He saw a name written across the first page. Fulcanelli. And he felt a sense of peace and acceptance. This was *his* book. *His* writing. *His* name. He really *was* Fulcanelli.

He flicked the pages forward. And as the pages turned, Jed saw words he recognised. Phrases he remembered.

Then the pages stopped turning.

It was here. The recipe to the elixir of eternal life. They'd found it.

Suddenly, the sky exploded with light. Fireworks rocketed up from the ground, shattering the sky into colour and flame.

Down in the courtyard, the revellers were celebrating the end of the Festival of Fools. But it was nothing in comparison to the celebration Jed would have with his friends. Their search was over. They'd found what they were looking for.

\* \* \*

Jed could never remember feeling so happy. Excitement and relief flowed through his veins. He tried to process the feeling that felt the strongest. Satisfaction. They'd done what they'd come all this way to do.

It was true the recipe was just the beginning. The elixir still had to be made. But hope came from the truth that now he would know how.

The whole journey had been one of questions and puzzles that needed solving. And finally he held the answer in his hands. For the first time since he'd climbed out of the Thames in London, Jed felt complete.

The book wasn't heavy. Small really, but the size of its importance was unfathomable. This tiny manuscript opened up all sorts of possibilities that he'd never even allowed himself to think about before. A future. Life beyond the confines of a calendar year.

And Kassia.

If Jed was really going to be fully cured of death now, then perhaps there was a chance for them to be *normal*. Maybe he could open up to her like he'd never done before.

He hadn't been able to take the risk until now. What did he have to offer her, when his time could be counted in months? But now there would be no limits. Time would be stretched. Everything would be different, and everything would be possible.

Jed looked for a moment beyond the edge of the tower balcony. He could see the whole of Paris sparkling in the strengthening light of the moon and a rainbow of fireworks. Golden rain splashed down on the Eiffel Tower and spilled across the surface of the Seine. The tower, a bigger and more brilliant version of the one in Petřín; the river a wider, deeper version of the Vltava. It struck Jed that rivers acted as markers to his adventure. From the Thames, to the Neckar, to the Vltava and finally the Seine, the four rivers completed the edges of a square and brought him back to the thing that had begun his journey in the first place. Life victorious over death. The rivers were like ink that flowed to tell his story. And now the ink had written that he would truly live forever. The hope that surged inside him was the strongest thing he'd ever felt.

He looked across at Jacob, who'd been with him on the journey. Jacob held both torches in his hands and the flames danced either side of his reddened face. His eyes were wide. Full of understanding. The journey was over now.

Jacob looked down at his hands as if he wanted to be free of the fire. Then he took both torches, angling them sideways and jabbing them hard into the open mouth of the gargoyle dragon. The flames twisted and spluttered, rearranging their burning so that the two torches looked like one flaming log wedged across the dragon's jaw. The dragon was breathing fire. As if it was as alive as Jed felt.

Jacob turned away from the gargoyle and wiped his sooty hands on his suit. Then he reached up and pulled the rubber skull cap from his head. He looked like a snake shedding its skin. His face was strangely distorted now, greasepaint smudged, his features undefined.

Another cloud of fireworks exploded above them and in the falling sparks, Jacob's eyes flashed wildly. The fire from the dragon's mouth behind him leapt and stretched in the firelight and Jacob looked more beastlike than some of the stone animals that guarded the cathedral. Somehow, not fully human.

'Can I see the book?' Jacob said, tossing the skull-cap mask to the ground.

Jed watched the mask tumble along the walkway. It looked like a decapitated head and Jed felt weirdly squeamish. And he felt something else too. A powerful emotion that pushed up from his stomach. The book was his. Both in the past, because he'd written it, and now. He didn't want to hand it over.

'The book?' Jacob said again. 'Can I see?'

Jed tightened his grip on the leather covers. Not yet.

The sky was ripped apart again by an explosion of fire and for the first time, Jed was able to get a better sense of where they were in relation to the rest of the building. The bell towers rose higher than the roof of the cathedral. If he walked along the balcony, he would be able to reach the front and look down into the courtyard on the clowns at the Festival. He could also see that the walkway stretched along the back of the cathedral. The whole route, stretching round both turrets, was protected by the metal fencing. Jed looked across. Kassia and Dante were searching there now, with no idea the book had been found. The door to their tower was closed and there was clearly no handle on the outside. It must mean that the doors locked when shut. If this hadn't been so, then this entrance would have been the best way to reach them.

Behind the two towers, and slightly lower, the huge pitched roof of the cathedral strained upwards. At the far end of this roof and opposite the towers was a tall spire. In the flash of fireworks, Jed could see that metal statues of men marked the edge of the cathedral roof and made a procession line, spreading towards the base of the spire.

There was another explosion of light. A metal rooster,

which must have been some sort of weather vane, spun on the tip of the spire, glowing red as it turned.

Jed heard footsteps. Jacob had begun to walk along the balcony. He stopped at the doorway they'd used to get outside. Maybe seeing that the other door was closed, Jacob was going to run down the stairs, and tell Kassia and Dante the search was over. But Jacob didn't walk through the doorway. Instead, he reached out for the wooden prop that was jammed in the hinges, keeping the door open.

'Woah, steady!' Jed called. 'Don't take that out. If that door locks shut, we'll be trapped up here.'

Jacob didn't turn. He yanked the prop from its position. The door, which was their only exit from the balcony back into the tower, slammed shut.

Only then did Jacob look towards him. 'Hand me the book,' he said.

Jed was confused.

What was Jacob doing?

Jed moved quickly to the now closed door and rammed his shoulder hard against it. It was locked. No give at all. 'What did you do that for? How are we going to get down?'

Jacob held the wooden prop across his body and was tipping each end up and down in his palms as if checking the weight of a weapon. 'Maybe I don't want to go down the tower. Yet,' he said.

'What?' Jed had no idea what was happening. Jacob's eyes were wide, the red paint smudged down the lower part of his face; the top of his head free now of the mask and wig, slick with sweat.

'You have quite some treasure in your hand there,' Jacob said sharply. 'And we came here for treasure after all. So I think it's time you handed it over, don't you?'

Why did Jacob want him to hand the book over? Why couldn't he wait? None of this was making sense.

'I get the treasure is important to *you*, Jed. We *all* know how important the recipe is to you! We've been trailing round the whole of Europe, day and night, because *you* need to make the elixir,' he hesitated for a moment. 'But did you ever stop to think about how important it is to other people?' He shook his head slowly. 'I didn't think so.'

Suddenly, Jacob swung the end of the wooden prop forward. Jed lurched backwards, recoiling as the end of the prop whipped past his stomach. Why was Jacob trying to hit him? What was the matter with the man? Jed sank down to his knees and crawled along the walkway, clutching the book tight to his chest. Above him, the metal fencing glinted under another explosion of fireworks. He was in a cage again. Trapped by someone who suddenly seemed to have lost his mind.

'The secret in that book gives the chance to be in control,' Jacob went on, swinging the wooden prop as he walked so that it bounced against the wall of the balcony, plaster and brick-dust cascading down as a result of each strike. 'Can you even begin to get your head round the value of what we've found here?' The end of the prop bashed against the wall. A cloud of dust lifted and dispersed.

Value? What was Jacob talking about? The recipe was to stop Jed dying. That's why they were here.

Jacob drove the prop down to the ground as if it was a staff carried by a wizard about to attempt some incredible magic. 'Think of the possibilities here, Jed. How we could work together in this. You and me. We wouldn't ever have to be victims of chance again. We could have power. The proper kind. Do you see that?'

This talk of power was scaring Jed. He scrambled up from the floor and pushed the book deep into his pocket. There was no way he would let Jacob get his hands on the recipe now. Not while he was behaving so manically.

But the sight of Jed hiding the book only enraged Jacob. He drilled the prop down again on to the ground. 'Have you ever lost anyone, Jed?'

Jed's mind flung him back to the river bank in

Heidelberg, watching Kassia fight for her life. But being here wasn't about memories or what was past. It was about the present and the future and what he wanted now was to get away. But both doors to the towers were locked. There was no way down. He scrambled along the balcony. He could hear Jacob striding after him. But there was no urgency in his pace. Because Jacob could see what Jed could see. The caging had dead-ended, making it impossible to walk all the way around the balcony. Eventually, Jed would be cornered. There would be no escape.

Jed grabbed hold of the metal caging. He'd no idea what to do. He backed further down the walkway. Jacob was closing in. The wooden prop was raised again; his shoulders back in preparation to make another swing.

Jed glanced down at the fall from the balcony. The pitched roof of the cathedral strained upwards, like the sail of a ship. Jacob was getting closer, the wooden prop swinging. Jed needed time to think this through. But there was no time! In seconds, Jacob would be close enough to wrestle the book from him. And then what? Would Jacob even let Jed see the recipe if he wanted it so desperately for himself? Would all the searching be for nothing?

Jed's fingers fumbled on the metal. And then

slipped free of the bars. There was a gap! A tiny space, between the edge of the caging and the wall of the tower. A gap just big enough to squeeze through.

'Have you ever lost someone?' Jacob shouted again. 'Felt your insides ripped out as you watched them slip away from you?'

Jed saw the paramedics shocking Kassia's heart. And he felt his own heart tearing inside of him. But this was about now. Not then. He looked again at the breach in the fencing and out into the space behind the tower. Below was the pitched roof of the back section of the cathedral. Jacob was getting closer. Jed's mind was spinning. Did he wait it out? But how could he keep the book safe? Maybe there was another way down. Windows below the pitched roof, he could climb through into the cathedral if he could reach them.

'Have you ever felt totally powerless?' Jacob yelled. 'While something you knew you couldn't change crept closer and closer?'

Jed remembered realising he only had a year to find the elixir. The time bomb ticking out every step they took. But Jacob wasn't talking about that, was he?

Jacob swung again with the prop. Another cloud of brick-dust lifted from the wall as the end of the wooden staff bashed against it.

Jed stared through the opening in the wire. The roof was metres below them. He was certainly feeling powerless now. But did that mean he should give the book over to Jacob?

Jed clambered up into the space in the fencing. He balanced himself on the edge of the balcony wall, his legs tucked, his weight poised.

Jacob saw too late what Jed was going to do. Jacob lurched forward, the wooden prop swinging in his hand. But the stick caught only the edge of the fencing. 'Give me the book!' he yelled. 'I refuse to feel powerless again.'

Jed flung himself forward, away from the tower. He reached his hands out, spread-eagled his body and braced himself for impact. And as he flew through the air towards the pitched roof below, he screamed only one word. 'NO!'

Jed's stomach thumped hard against the roof. Air blasted out of his lungs. He scrabbled with his fingers to latch on to the ridge, his fingers slipping and slithering. He grabbed hold. Then he tried to breathe.

This was total madness! He was clambering on the roof of Notre Dame Cathedral. But everything had changed. Minutes before, he'd been bathing in the brilliance of knowing he'd discovered the recipe for the elixir. And now he was being hunted down by someone who wanted the book for himself. Worst of all, that someone was a *friend*. Someone Jed had trusted and travelled with. Someone who was supposed to be there to help him.

'You're not keen to share your treasure then, I take it,' Jacob bellowed across the gap between the balcony and the roof. 'Shame that.' He struck the wall of the balcony again with the end of the wooden prop. 'Because I would have been willing to share. I'm a reasonable man. But you see, death isn't reasonable, is it? It's vicious and indiscriminate. And that's not right, Jed. I finally have the chance to use the power to make things right. And I'm not going to let you stop me.'

Jed was clinging desperately to the ridge of the roof. His feet were kicking against the tiles, scratching for a better hold. His heart was hammering in his chest. The book, a sharp block against his leg, dug into his thigh.

Jacob hit the balcony wall again with the prop and then let out a groan. He tossed the prop aside and hauled himself up into the opening in the wire fencing, crouched down low and hoisted himself forward. He was going to jump too! Fling himself on to the roof just like Jed had done.

'Did you know I had a brother?' Jacob yelled, his hands gripping tight to the edge of the fencing. 'Of course you didn't! Because *that's* the issue. You don't know a single thing about me, do you?'

Was that true? Jed wasn't sure. He remembered Jacob had been in a graffiti crew. He'd said that once. But a brother? Family? He'd never mentioned them. But what had this got to do with anything? Why was this important now? And why had the man he'd trusted suddenly turned against him so that he was hanging metres above the ground on a rooftop in central Paris?

Jacob scrunched his body forwards, braced himself and then launched himself on to the roof. The sleeve of his too-big suit caught on the metal, ripping and flapping free as he landed spread-eagled on the tiles.

Jed lifted hand over hand and edged his way along the roofing and away from the towers and towards the spire. What did he do now? How could he get away?

Jacob hauled himself up the slates, both hands gripping tightly to the roof ridge. Jacob was facing certain death if he fell. But he didn't look scared. He looked angry.

Jed scrabbled against the roof tiles. It was clear now he was too high above the windows. There was no way he could clamber down the roof and then swing into the building. He'd thrown himself from the balcony in an attempt to get away and all he'd done was make everything a hundred times worse.

Jacob hoisted himself up, clambering so that he straddled the ridge of the roof as if he was riding a horse. Then he pulled himself up to stand. Fireworks lit the sky behind him. 'My brother was a good man!' he shouted. 'The very best of men.' He rocked backwards, his arms stretched wide like a tightrope walker. 'But life had other plans for him,' he yelled. 'Or should I say, death had other plans.' He leaned forward and looked for a moment as if he was going to topple.

Jed moved his hands again, one over the other. The end of the roof was drawing closer. The spire, and the statues of the climbing men, getting nearer. He just needed to steady himself, so he could think. Work out what to do.

Jacob began to step along the roof ridge. 'Ask me about my brother, Jed! Go on! Ask me.'

One more swing of his hand and Jed would be able to reach the base of the spire. Then he'd have time to think!

Jacob yelled out into the night as a cloud of fireworks exploded above them. 'He died!'

Jed's hand was on the base of the spire. He grabbed hard and flung himself forward, wrapping his arms around the widest part of the spire as if he was trying to hug it.

But Jacob hadn't finished. He was stepping forward; moving in. 'There was no magic elixir for him,' he yelled. 'No second chances. He'd never hurt a single soul but that wasn't enough. *I* wasn't enough. I've spent my life caring for others. A social worker!' he yelled. 'It's what I do. Care! So shouldn't there be some payback? Some balance!' He took a deep breath. 'The only thing my brother wanted, the one thing he needed, I couldn't give to him. I failed.' He flung his arms wide again as if the words were burning in his chest. 'I wasn't enough, Jed!'

Jed clung tight to the base of the spire. He'd hoped there would be some ledges or framework here, at the end of the building, leading to windows below the line of the roofing. Something he could grip on to as he climbed down. Spaces he could swing into. A route inside. But there was nothing. He'd worked his way into another trap. There was nowhere to go and Jacob was inching nearer!

'But I could be now!' Jacob yelled. 'This could be about *me* for once in my life. I could be the one who makes the decisions. Because that recipe is not something you should keep to yourself. It's not fair! You alone holding the answer to death. You have to see that, Jed, don't you? This can't be just about you any more. I can't let that happen! I've been so patient.

But I can't wait any more. I can't fail again.'

Jacob had moved so far along the ridge, he was close enough to touch. Jed took a breath. He needed to move but he'd reached the end of the line. He'd no idea what to do. The only chance of escape was to get back on to the balcony. But he wasn't sure he had the strength to do that. His arm was shaking, his vision swimming. Maybe he could climb on to one of the statues? Use one of them as a place to get his breath, then work back towards the towers? He flung his leg out, tried to steady himself above the statue, but it was so far away, the perspective all wrong. His fingers were slipping. Another blast of fireworks like gun fire. He let go of the spire. The air burned red. He reached sideways and then tumbled free of the base of the spire, sliding down the roof. He drove his heels down hard against the tiles, but he was slipping and falling. He thrust his shoulders back. Scratched his fingernails against the roofing. Then he slammed hard into a statue of a climbing man.

On the ridge of the roof, Jacob was standing boldly, as if he was surfing on the crest of a wave. What was he doing? How was Jacob not falling?

'My brother taught me to do this. I'm what you call a free-runner. Scaling buildings was our thing. You think this little roof is going to scare me?' He laughed.

'Not now. Because I'm not scared any more. Of anything. Not even death.' He hesitated. 'Because if you give me that book I can finally be in control. I can make decisions about who death claims. And I will make things fair!'

Jed's arms were straining, buckling under the pressure of holding on.

'Good catch, by the way,' Jacob said, gesturing towards the statue Jed was desperately clinging on to. 'Kind of ironic you're holding on to a statue of St Thomas, don't you think? Of all the apostles climbing on this roof, he was the one who doubted.' He laughed again. 'I don't do doubt! That's not my style. I believe you will hand that book to me, Jed. Looks to me as if you've got yourself into rather a tight situation in your attempts to get away.' He waved his hands to the side and Jed lowered his head, scared to watch him fall. 'When I have that book, death will only come to those who deserve it. Not good people. Or kind people. Not people like my brother. You get that, don't you? You have no doubts about what this power could mean!'

What Jed was totally getting was that the man wasn't thinking straight. How could anyone possibly decide who was good enough to live or bad enough to die?

Fireworks shattered the sky, illuminating the line of

statue apostles that processed along the roof edge towards the spire.

As the sparks thundered down, Jed lowered his head. Memories came flashing back to him. Not confined within the framing of a dragon this time, but new memories unframed and un-dulled.

And with sickening clarity, Jed finally understood.

This wasn't sudden madness. Jacob hadn't snapped or turned. Jacob had betrayed him. Not just now, as he clawed his way across a rooftop and tried to take something he believed should be his. But before that. In Prague. This had all been planned.

Jed remembered the astronomical clock. They'd stood and watched the apostles appear and parade around the time piece, just as the apostles paraded here on this rooftop. Andel had mentioned Judas. The ultimate betrayer. And Jacob had stumbled where he stood. He must have been working with Andel. Had given away their secret to the old man from the House of the Stone Ram and that's how NOAH had found them.

And being here, just the two of them on the tower. This was all part of the plan to make sure he was alone with Jed when the book was found. Jacob had never had any intention of letting Jed keep the recipe for himself.

Jed felt as if he'd been kicked in the stomach. But there was no time to think this through. Jacob had made it to the end of the roof ridge. In seconds he'd be close enough to the spire to work his way down the edge of the roof to where Jed was hanging on.

So this betrayal was planned, then. Worked out in advance, was it? Two could play at being prepared!

Jed braced his arms and dug down deep inside himself. Then, as the cockerel weather vane spun above them in the wind, Jed threw himself forward and clambered back up towards the spire. Jacob looked surprised. He hadn't expected Jed to move *towards* him. He hesitated for a moment as Jed climbed up past the spire and then down the far side of the pitch of the roof.

He was facing the other section of the balcony now. The North Tower. The only way to escape this madness was to work his way along the guttering of the roof and get back on to the balcony and hope that he could leave Jacob stranded.

Jed worked his way back towards the bell tower, his fingers slipping and sliding across the roof tiles. Fired by desperation to get away, he braced himself and looked up at the wall of the balcony. But on this side he could see no gap in the fencing to aim for. Maybe the metal cage was the solution.

He glanced for a second, down across the gulf between the roof and the balcony. It had been one thing to jump *down* on to the roof. But could he really scramble *up* on to the balcony? There was only one way to find out.

He scrunched his body, flexed his shoulders, then pushed off against the roof. A tile skittered free. He did not hear it crash to the ground. The fall was too far.

There was a second where Jed was flying. Then the metal wire of the fencing bashed against his face. He scratched to get hold. Breath stuttered in his throat. He'd made it. He was on the outside of the balcony but he needed to be inside the cage. It was almost laughable. Months ago he'd escaped from a cage, and now he was fighting to get back inside one.

He hauled himself up the caging, jabbing his feet into the gaps between the bars until he was able to clamber up on to the top of the network of metal that ran along the length of the walkway. Surely he could find a way in from here? His weight was buckling the wire. He shook the bars. Rammed his hands down hard. There was a rupturing sound. A fixing levered loose from the wall of the tower. Jed slumped to the side. The caging buckled further. More fixings pinged loose. Then he swayed to his left as the caging folded in on itself and he fell on to the ground of the balcony. He'd done it. He was back on the other side from where he'd started. But back on the tower section of the cathedral.

Behind him, he could hear Jacob scaling the roof. Running across the tiles. He was good at this. Knew what he was doing. At this rate it wouldn't be long before he'd made it across the gap too and was back at the tower.

So Jed had to get to the doorway before that happened. The door to the opposite tower was locked. But things were more desperate now. He'd have to break it down.

Jed ran along the balcony. Getting closer with every step was the gargoyle dragon, mouth still clamped on the burning torches, flames still belching from its throat.

Jed reached the door. He thumped his shoulder hard against it, just like Jacob had done to the door at the bottom of the tower. Nothing. But Jed was angry now. Fury surged inside him. He slammed his shoulder again and again against the door. And then another memory jolted into view. The withered hand, hanging in the street in Prague. Warning of a thief.

Jed was incensed. He shoulder-barged one final time at the door. There was the sound of splintering.

The door buckled, shook for a moment and fell from its hinges.

The door was open. There was a way out.

But a hand clamped hard on Jed's shoulder and tugged him out of the way, sending him spilling on his back and skidding along the walkway of the balcony. His spine thudded hard against the wall. He'd landed at the foot of the stone dragon. Sparks billowed from the flaming torches gripped tight between the stone monster's jaws. And Jacob stood, just metres away, amongst the tangled mess of fallen fencing.

And in the light of a burst of fireworks, Jacob reached out his hand and made a grab for Jed.

Jed noticed for the very first time the design of the tattoo that circled up Jacob's arm, visible now because the sleeve of the clown suit had ripped away. It was of a unicorn. And around the foot of the unicorn was a chain.

Words and memories collided in Jed's mind. And the truth he saw then was more painful and more repulsive than anything else he'd managed to work out on the rooftop.

That's what NOAH had called Jed. A unicorn. And that's what they'd done to him. Kept him in chains. Jed had seen the same tattoo on Cole's arm when he'd been questioned back in London. And now Jacob wore the symbol as a badge of honour. He'd switched sides. Not just in Prague, but before that. On the Devil's Stone. NOAH hadn't beaten and abandoned Jacob in the woods. They'd captured and converted him. The bandage on his arm hadn't been wrapped around a wound. It had hidden the mark of his allegiance to the other side.

Jacob's betrayal had been carefully planned. But worse than all of that was that the man who'd pretended to help them had actually been part of NOAH after all.

'HAND ME THE BOOK!' Jacob was bellowing. His eyes wide, his face streaked with paint.

Jed backed against the wall, his body curled inwards in an attempt to keep the book safe.

How could he hand the recipe over to a man who wanted to be the one to make decisions about the life and death of others? A man who was sure he could decide who was good enough to be immortal? What would he do? Charge for the recipe? Test people to see if they deserved to live or die? Turn survival into a business where only the richest could afford to prove they were good enough to keep breathing? The ultimate apartheid, NOAH had said. Those who had life and those who didn't. And Jacob wanted to be the dictator.

Jacob reached down, grabbed Jed and pulled him upwards, then flung him hard so that his back crunched against the wall. 'Give me the book!'

If Jacob had the recipe, then there was still a chance he'd let Jed make the elixir for himself. There was still a chance Jed would have the *forever* and the *normal* that he craved. Jacob had talked about working together. It didn't mean that Jed would lose the elixir.

But at what cost?

Jed fumbled in his pocket. He took the book and held it out. 'You want this?' he said. 'You want to be the one to make the choices? You want to have the power over life and death?'

'Isn't that what *you* wanted?' Jacob growled.

Maybe. Yes. But not to make divisions between who was good enough to go on living and who wasn't.

Handing Jacob the chance to control the knowledge of the elixir would do worse than make him a dictator. It would turn him into a god. A vicious god, who wanted to make the decisions about who had the right to live or die. Should a man who'd been damaged by the loss of a brother make that decision? Should *anyone* make that decision?

The sky was suddenly dark. The fireworks, for a moment, set on pause.

Jed knew he couldn't give Jacob the recipe. Even if

that meant, after all his searching and all his struggles, losing the elixir for himself.

Jed steadied himself against the wall of the balcony. The fire burned bright in the mouth of the stone dragon.

He had only one choice left to him.

He reached out with his free hand and tugged the burning torches from their resting place in the jaws of the gargoyle. Then he swung the torches through the air and pressed the flames against the edge of the book.

And the fire burned.

'What are you doing?' Jacob charged forward. But the book was already ablaze. The ancient pages snapping and curling, smoke billowing in great belching clouds. 'You idiot!'

Jacob flung himself on to Jed and the torches crashed from his hand, rolling and spinning along the walkway. But Jed held on to the book. He watched it burn and splutter, the answers to all his questions sparking with flame. His eyes stung with tears; not just from the soot and the smoke but from the agony of seeing his hopes turn to ash in his hands.

Jacob flung Jed again into the wall of the balcony. The last loosened fencing of the cage buckled and twisted, the line of protection collapsing around them. Still Jed held the burning book; the flames biting closer to his fingers.

'Give it to me!' Jacob yelled again, flinging his arm wide and lurching outwards.

Jed's back was pinned to the wall of the balcony. He twisted and faltered as Jacob hurled himself forward, his eye on the prize.

Jacob's feet caught on the mangled, metal caging on the ground. This propelled him upwards, like a catapult, turning him in the air so he was carried over the wall. His stomach crashed against the brickwork on the outside edge of the balcony. His hands clung desperately to the top edge of the wall. The drop down to the courtyard in front of the cathedral was fully exposed and Jacob was suspended above it.

There was a moment of clarity, framed by the light of the flames.

Jed flung one hand to the side, releasing the burning book so it skidded along the wide expanse of the top of the wall. The fire burned and spluttered as the ball of flames twisted and spun, then settled on the wall, blazing like a beacon just above where Jacob was dangling.

Jacob was clinging on. His fingernails latched on to the plaster; his feet kicking madly at the wall.

'Hang on,' yelled Jed, rushing towards him.

Jacob swung one hand free of the wall and grabbed

Jed's arm. His nails dug into Jed's skin; his weight wrenching against Jed's shoulder.

Jed braced himself. His knees were digging hard, his stomach was cutting into the edge of the thick expanse of wall.

Jacob's chest was heaving, his feet kicking wildly. He was screaming. And the word he screamed was 'why?'

Why had Jed set the book on fire when it was his only hope of staying alive? Why was he holding on to Jacob when the man had tried to take everything away from him? Jed knew the answers, but he had no breath to speak them. He could only scream for Jacob to hang on.

'Take my other hand!' Jed yelled, as the noise from the finale of the Festival engulfed them.

Jacob's hand was slipping from the ledge on the wall. His fingers peeling away from their hold, one by one.

'My other hand!' Jed yelled again, and the top of the wall scored into his stomach as he leaned in tighter, Jacob's weight tugging him forward.

And Jacob stared at him. His eyes looked different now. Not wild. Not even scared. Determined.

'Now!' Jed yelled, willing Jacob to grab on to his other arm so he could pull him over the wall to safety.

And Jacob let go of the wall, so that for a second he was swinging just in Jed's hold. But he didn't reach out to grab Jed's other hand. Instead, his fingers lurched across for the blazing book on the top of the wall.

The reach was too far. The flames swelled in one final burst of energy just as the sky was ripped apart by an explosion of fireworks, bigger and louder than any Jed had ever seen.

Jacob's eyes locked on Jed's. His flailing hand banged against the bricks. The hand in Jed's grasp slipped. The fingers strained. Jed tried to hang on. But Jacob's fingers slid again, his free hand too far wide now to steady him.

Jacob's eyes closed. And his fingers began to open.

Notre-Dame -
...aul II,
...s, France

stall them, so NOAH could close in.

'But before that too, probably,' Jed went on. 'The Devil's Stone. Maybe even before that. I think him using his credit card in Heidelberg was how NOAH found us by the Neckar.'

Kassia sank back on to her heels. Had Jacob ever been on their side, then? His offer of a home in London. The getaway to Spain. Had that all been part of a plan to wear Jed down? 'But why?' she blurted. 'Why pretend to be our friend, if he was really one of them?'

'Power,' said Jed.

Kassia wasn't sure what he meant.

'He wanted the power to decide who could live or die,' Jed said. 'That's what it came down to in the end.' He covered his face for a moment and she could see that his hand was trembling, as if his whole arm was no longer under his control. He clutched it still with his other hand and looked at the ground. He was embarrassed. And in a desperate attempt to make things better, she leant forward and touched his shoulder reassuringly. She could feel the heat pumping out through his jumper.

'I tried to hold on to him,' he blurted. 'Tried to pull him back over the wall. But he wanted the book. He was stretching out . . .'

'The book!' Kassia's heart was racing. 'It was there! You found it!'

Jed tried to make his face into a smile but it did not reach his eyes. 'It was there.'

'And it had the recipe?' she urged, frantic now to hear the details.

'It had the recipe.'

'Well that's great! That's fantastic!' Nothing else mattered then. The betrayal. The deceit. The wasted time. If they had the recipe then everything was going to be OK.

Jed moved where he sat, his face even closer to hers, their foreheads almost touching 'It's gone,' he said.

'What do you mean, gone?'

'Burned. Turned to dust.'

Anger swelled again inside her. 'Jacob did that?' she yelled, pulling away. Rage pulsed through her veins. Jacob had tricked them, lied to them, deceived them. And then he'd burned the thing they searched for. The thing that would help Jed live. The thing that would make everything possible.

She tried to stand, as if the crouched position was too hunched over to contain the rage that filled her. But Jed tugged her down again, his face so close now that she could feel his breath on her cheeks.

'I burned the book,' he said.

'What? Why?'

'He was going to take the recipe and sell it!' Jed pleaded. 'I couldn't let that happen!'

'But what about you? What about the cure? How will we make the elixir now?' she spluttered, and tears smarted in her eyes.

'I don't know,' he said, and his whole body was shaking.

Kassia slumped to the ground. A strand of her hair brushed against his cheek. Her eyes locked on his. She held her breath.

'You came back,' he said.

She nodded. Then she bit the edge of her lip to stop her voice from shaking as she answered him. 'I should never have left,' she said.


Victor looked down at his hands. They were lined with sweat. Suddenly a voice came from beside him. 'Mr Montgomery will see you now.'

Victor got up from the chair and walked back into the boardroom. Montgomery seemed to be standing just where he'd left him, his hands pressed against a map of Paris, spread across the table. He looked up and acknowledged Victor's presence. 'Carter not with you?'

'No, sir. He's back in the city. Trying to "smoke

him out", like you want.'

Montgomery laughed. 'Yes. That's what I want, Victor. It's all I want. Fulcanelli found.'

Victor shuffled his shoe across the thick-piled carpet. They didn't have this sort of stuff in Etkin House.

'I wanted to talk a little about what happened,' Montgomery said. 'About the collateral damage at the cathedral.'

Victor saw the hanging man in his head and tried to blink the image away. 'Carter said he was on our side,' said Victor.

'He was,' sighed Montgomery. 'Eventually. Everyone has their tipping point, you see. Jacob's was a common one.' He walked around the edge of the table so that he was closer to Victor, his voice more hushed. 'You saw what happened?'

'It was dark. It was a long way up.'

Montgomery laughed. 'It was murder, Victor. You do know that. You know that in that moment, Fulcanelli upped the stakes. He changed the rules completely. He killed to keep his secret. And that means we can stop at nothing now, absolutely nothing, to get answers.'

Victor looked down again at the carpet. The pattern swam before his eyes. He remembered the train in

Prague. How he had seen something in Fulcanelli's eyes just before he'd let him go.

'He's a cold-blooded killer and he's going to live for ever. He has to be stopped. I just wanted to check you understood.' He moved away again and this time he walked towards a small cabinet set on the wall beside the window. He turned the latch and opened the door. 'I also wanted to congratulate you, Victor. On your commitment to our cause. Carter said you were very brave. Very resourceful.'

Victor could hear blood pulsing in his ears.

Montgomery took two items from the cabinet. A small silver object shaped like a revolver. And a vial of ink. 'Your time has come, Victor. And you deserve it. You've earned it.' He turned and held his hands out so that Victor could see more clearly. 'The moment to be marked. To signify, now the stakes have been raised, just exactly whose side you're on.'

Jed was suddenly aware that he and Kassia were no longer alone. It was true that crowds of people had been making their way across the bridge since he'd first been here. But these people had kept away; skirting past, not getting too close. Separate as they were, amongst the crowd, there'd been a moment of something that felt like how he thought peace would feel. He'd thought then, that maybe things would be OK. But when he'd lifted his hand to sweep away a strand of hair that hung between them, his arm had convulsed and trembled.

Now even the fragment of peace they'd had was shattered. Someone had drifted out of the crowd and was making right towards them.

Jed staggered upwards and pulled Kassia with him, pressing his quivering arm around her and making his own body a block between her and the intruder.

Then he saw that the intruder was Dante.

Dante dropped the bags at his feet then held his hands up as a gesture of apology. Jed could almost see Kassia's heart racing and hadn't he promised the doctor back in Heidelberg he would look after her heart? He wasn't sure he had managed to keep that promise.

Dante lowered his hands and whipped them into sign. Jed's brain was a little rusty. He struggled to keep up and, as if sensing this, Kassia spoke the signs aloud. 'I don't know what happened on Notre Dame,' Dante signed. 'But my sister says you didn't kill Jacob and that's good enough for me.'

Jed was sure he could detect a tiny hesitation in Kassia's translation and it was this that magnified the hurt. For Dante then, Kassia's insistence of Jed's innocence had been enough. Words had not been enough for her, though.

Jed tried to smile, but as he turned to the side he saw that Kassia's face was pained too. She mouthed the word 'sorry', as if she understood what she had done when she had refused to believe him. More than anything, Jed wanted that to be enough, but he wasn't sure yet that it was. His heart was hurting now.

Dante was signing again, and this time Kassia offered no voiceover. Maybe she was scared of what her brother would say next. But Dante was just keen for them to move away from the bridge. It seemed he'd noticed people were watching them, and they couldn't risk any unwanted attention. He reminded Jed of the police crawling around Notre Dame. And of NOAH. What had happened should make them more vigilant, not less.

Jed nodded and together the three of them made their way to the end of the bridge and back on to the pavement. They found a flight of stairs that led down to the lower walkway stretching beside the Seine. There were spindly trees growing here and they stood beside the tallest one as if sheltering from rain.

Between them, Jed and Kassia tried to bring Dante up to speed. Dante winced as Jed tried to show how he'd struggled to hold on to Jacob's slipping hand. How he'd begged him to hang on. And how he'd fallen.

Dante looked uncomfortable throughout the whole explanation and Jed reasoned that he must feel Jacob's deception worst of all.

'So it's just the three of us, then,' said Dante at last, as if he wanted not to mention Jacob again, and as if that part was dealt with. 'Police will be after us. And NOAH. And we still haven't got the book you wrote. Things aren't looking too brilliant, are they?'

If it wasn't so desperate, it would have been funny. 'Yeah, it could be better,' said Jed. 'I mean, you're not only on the run with an immortal now, but also a suspect in a murder case. I like to do what I can to make life interesting.'

Kassia was smiling. 'You've certainly done that,' she said. 'Can't call any of this boring.'

Dante laughed. And Jed did too. For a moment it relieved the tension, and then Dante asked a question that brought the agony of what they were facing crashing back towards them like a runaway train. 'What about the book?' he signed.

Jed knew that Kassia was watching him. It wouldn't be any easier to tell her brother what he'd done than it had been to tell her. 'I burnt it,' he said.

Dante's face was a picture worth more than a

thousand words. So he didn't bother with all the questions that Kassia had tried.

'We wasted our time coming here,' said Jed, desperate to fill the silence and the stillness left by Dante's unmoving hands. 'We're no closer to making the elixir. In fact, we're further away. And now we have less than nine months left before—'

Kassia reached out and stopped his hands from making shapes. And the words died unuttered in his mouth. There was no need to say them aloud. They knew what this meant. Without the recipe for the elixir, what was there to pursue? All their striving had been about finding out what Fulcanelli had taken years to fathom. And now all that was known was lost.

'So what do we do?' said Kassia.

And in that moment, Jed forgave her the doubt and the confusion of days ago. She'd asked what *they* should do. Not *him*. Even after everything, they were still in this together.

'We try and get back to London,' offered Jed. 'I don't know if the passports will be blocked. I'm not sure if they've actually worked out it was me who was on the tower or if they're just searching for a man who was with Jacob when he fell. In London, maybe being with Anna and Nat will make things feel better for you. As we wait.'

'I'm not interested in making me feel better,' blurted Kassia. 'I'm interested in making *you* better! Curing you totally. The sixth elixir. That's what this is all about and any plans we make are about trying to find that, not choosing somewhere to go and sit and wait until the year's up.'

He felt a warmth flood through him.

'And the answers aren't in London, are they?'

'But we don't know what we're looking for now. Another version of the recipe? Some of the elixir itself? How would we know what to look for and where?'

'What about your home in Paris?' signed Dante.

'Too risky,' said Jed. He'd thought about that as he'd pounded the streets of the city at night. NOAH would have agents based there. It was where they'd expect him to go. He'd just be walking into their trap.

A tour boat glided past them on the river, the tinny commentary and some rambling explanation of the lovelock bridge, no doubt, drifting towards them in lilting French.

Kassia was looking across at the tour boat nervously. Jed could tell she was growing anxious. They were certainly more hidden here than on the bridge itself, but if they were really determined to keep out of the sight of NOAH, then the three of them being out in the open air together, anywhere at all, so close to the cathedral, was pushing things a bit.

'We just need somewhere quiet to go,' said Jed. 'So we can try and unravel this mess and find a new beginning.' But he'd run dry of ideas. It was impossible to work out what to do next. He had no inkling of where to go. And he was pretty sure they'd never find a solution to the mess that they were in.

They sat on the edge of the walkway, their feet dangling over the Seine. The water was rushing forwards, charging away from the cathedral. And Kassia knew that they should be doing that too. Putting as much distance between them and the scene of Jacob's death as possible. But none of them knew where to go. They were frozen. Trapped by tiredness and indecision.

Kassia looked up at Jed. He was staring down at the water, as if searching for his reflection there. If the water stilled enough to show him, the face he saw would be changed. Lines had deepened; a thick mauve bruise skirting the skin beneath each eye looked as thin as tissue paper. And the eyes themselves looked duller, as if the spark they'd had back in London – when they'd first ventured out of the house and bought steaming hot chocolate from a street vendor – had been diluted. She wanted to reach out and hug him. But he sat with his hands in his lap staring at the water and she wasn't sure if she should. Wasn't sure if he would want her to.

She pushed her own hands deep into her trouser pockets. She turned the coins there over and over, so they jangled together. The noise was soothing.

There was something in her pocket, though, that was silent. Not a coin at all, although it was equal to the coins in size. It was the package Giseppi had given her. She held it and it felt reassuring, despite its silence.

Kassia thought back to Giseppi and how he'd helped them. And how he'd changed too. On *The Phoenix* train out of Prague, she'd met a clown. But at the foot of Notre Dame, he'd turned into their protector. She thought back to how he'd taken them, without question or hesitation, to the Court of Miracles. And then she remembered their conversation when he'd left. It was almost as if he'd been guiding her to look more carefully at the photograph in the newspaper. As if he'd anticipated the miracle of her seeing Jacob clearly through his disguise as a friend.

Kassia's hand gripped tightly to the paper-clad coin Giseppi had given her. *Look more carefully.* Why hadn't she even unwrapped the thing to see what it was?

She tugged the package from her pocket and peeled back the folds of paper. A small copper disc tumbled into her lap. But it was not a coin.

'What is that?' signed Dante.

Kassia turned the disc over and over. On the top was a tiny raised loop, for a chain perhaps, used to turn the disc into a medallion. It was plain on one side, polished to a shine. But on the front of the disc was an engraving. A circle, within a square, within a triangle. The mark of the Brothers of Heliopolis. Giseppi obviously wanted Kassia to be certain she knew about his connections to the Brotherhood. But the medallion was more than just a reminder of his tattoo. It was familiar in another way too, which she couldn't quite work out.

Dante held out his hand and Kassia passed the disc over. The pain in his eyes seemed to have sharpened, as if he recognised the disc and not just the symbol, too.

'Who gave you that?' Jed asked.

'Giseppi. I think he is a modern Brother of Heliopolis, if it's even possible to be one of those. He had a tattoo of the symbol on his shoulder.'

Kassia could see Jed was trying to process this information. But she was sure he was thinking about another tattoo as well.

Dante handed the disc back and began to sign. 'You think they still exist?'

'Maybe. There was a list of the names of the original Brothers in the Court of Miracles. And—' She wanted to tell them. About the name she'd seen and how maybe their grandfather had been involved with Fulcanelli when he'd first made the elixir. But there wasn't time. Jed had stood up. He was agitated; his leg trembling.

'Court of Miracles. What's that?' Jed blurted.

'Where Giseppi took us. A place to hide.'

'So we should go back there. Find Giseppi again and ask him what he knows.'

'He's not there any more.'

'Where is he?' Jed urged.

Kassia scrabbled in her mind to find an answer. 'Somewhere quiet, he said. For a meeting.'

Dante grabbed for the paper Kassia had discarded when she'd unwrapped the medallion. 'What's this? Says something about a gasworks.'

Kassia scrambled up from the ground now too. 'That's it. He said, this was to help me find him if I needed to. That's where he's gone. Some laboratory in a gasworks. Maybe we should go there? Find out if he has any clue about the elixir?'

'Seems good to me,' signed Dante. 'We haven't any better ideas.'

Jed was nodding but he was obviously finding it hard to stand. 'Gasworks,' he said quietly.

Kassia knew what he was getting at. When Jed had

seen the gasworks in London from the top of the O2, he'd had a terrible reaction. The memories it provoked had made Jed collapse and he'd had to be carried down from the climb. 'This is different,' she said, trying to sound reassuring. 'This isn't London.'

Jed looked terrified. 'I know. It's Paris. And that might not be different in a good way.'

Jed took the piece of paper that had been used to wrap the medallion. He ran his eyes over the address that was printed there and then said the words aloud: 211, Avenue Jean-Jaurès. The words muddled in his mind and then, as if a cloud was lifting and the sky becoming clearer, a wisp of memory began to appear.

Jed was scared. He braced himself. He knew what would follow.

The dragon spun in his mind, round and round, dragging the wisp of memory, thickening and deepening it until a fully formed recollection filled the space.

Jed saw a laboratory. Glass vessels and containers glinted in the light of the sun, but the room was cold. Two men stood facing each other. An old man talking to a younger one. The old man was anxious. He was fiddling with his hands. His words were clipped and fast, and in French. And the young man was confused.

Scared even, by what he heard.

Jed clutched at his head and pulled away from the memory so that the body of the dragon dissolved and drifted away, like the blackened smoke that blazes from burning car tyres.

It was the same memory from the top of the O2. But this time the details were sharper.

Jed pressed his hands hard against his skull. The pain was overwhelming but he did not fall down this time.

Something momentous happened in that gasworks laboratory in Paris but Jed didn't have the strength to go deeper into the memory. He couldn't bear to remember what happened. Nor could he bear to work out why this memory, and not the recollections of a train crash, or the hurricane or all the memories he faced in Prague, felt the most dangerous of all.

He was aware that Kassia was looking at him. She was scared for him, but not as scared as he was for himself.

Dante took the paper and read the address, and as if he had decided to take on the mantle of being in charge now, he led them up the steps on to the higher walkway and raced across to the nearest street vendor.

The stallholder smiled as Dante approached. He looked him up and down as if mentally calculating the amount he was likely to spend, then selected a metal replica of the Eiffel Tower, two Notre Dame keyrings and a lovelock and pushed them forward across the table in front of him.

Dante shook his head and gestured to the line of guidebooks propped on a shelf behind him.

Dante handed over coins from his pocket and then flicked through the guidebook to the atlas section. Then he turned the page to the transport guide. Decision made, he gestured to Jed and Kassia to follow and raced off towards the metro station.

Jed was not keen to take a train. Things had not gone brilliantly well for them on their other train journeys. But Dante was not in the mood to discuss options. He selected coins for the machine, then collected the three tickets that spewed from it. They boarded a number 7 train bound for Gare de l'Est.

Once they'd found a seat, Kassia grabbed the guidebook. 'It says the gasworks was part of an industrial area across the city,' she signed, balancing the open book on her lap. 'There used to be slaughter houses there, as well as the gasworks.'

'Used to be?' pressed Jed.

'It says here that great areas of the gasworks and industrial spaces have been replaced,' Kassia added. The train lurched a little to the right and Jed slid closer towards her on the seat. Once the train had straightened, he didn't pull away.

'Why are we going to a place that no longer exists?' Jed asked quietly.

From her hesitation, it was clear that Kassia was trying her best to work out the answer. 'The place still *exists*. It's just changed. And Giseppi was keen I knew it was a gasworks laboratory in the past, I guess.'

The train pulled into the platform and Dante steered them across the station, leading the way on to a second train. 'We're aiming for Porte de Pantin,' he said, spelling out each letter needed for the destination.

The second train was less crowded. Kassia held the book closed now, all the details they needed gleaned from the pages she'd read. But Jed knew they needed more. He knew that he had to go back into the memory of the gasworks, to make sense of why a man they'd met on a train leaving Prague seemed so keen for them to know about a destination across the city.

Jed bit the inside of his lip. He wasn't sure he was brave enough for this. And then as if sensing what he was about to do, Kassia let her leg press against his. 'There's a memory?' she asked quietly.

'It really hurts,' said Jed. 'I'm not sure if I can.'

'I'll be with you,' she said gently and she reached out and offered him her hand.

Jed squeezed her hand tight and closed his eyes. He willed the dragon to swirl and, for a moment, he thought the memory would fail to return, as if it had been lost again as it must have been for years. But then the space behind his closed eyes darkened and the segmented body of a dragon dragged itself into the space created in his mind. And it began to spin. It twisted round and round, boring down through all the memories he knew about and all those that seemed out of reach. In the centre of the memory, sharper than on the O2 and sharper than earlier, Jed saw the old man and the younger man: the old man was frantic and he wasn't just twisting his hands together, he was wringing them, as if what he was saying was so important he wanted to wash all traces of the words from him. And the younger man was not just confused or scared this time. He was terrified.

Jed forced himself to look. Then, when the pain was so sharp it took his breath away, he blinked his eyes and looked down at his hand locked in Kassia's grasp. And he saw that his hands were the same as those in the memory. The old man in the memory was him.

Jed jerked his hand free of Kassia and pressed his fist against his mouth. He couldn't breathe. He knew that for the stories they'd worked out about him to be true, he must have been old before. But it was the first time he'd fully understood what that meant.

Kassia slipped down from the seat, so that she was kneeling in the gangway squarely in front of him, making it impossible for him to turn away from her. She stared up at him. 'Jed?'

'I can't,' he spluttered. 'It hurts too much.' How could he tell her what he'd seen?

'But do you understand the memory?' she whispered gently.

He shook his head and snatches of the image thumped around inside his skull, shattering into a thousand pieces. He looked up. 'Bergier,' he said. The younger man in the memory. He knew his name.

'What?'

'There's a man in the memory and his name was Bergier.'

'That's Giseppi's surname,' Kassia cried. 'Do you think he's a descendant of the man you can see?'

'Maybe?'

'And what's happening in the memory?'

'I'm talking to this Bergier guy. We're in a laboratory. In a gasworks, I suppose.'

'And what are you talking about?' Dante asked.

Jed had no idea how to explain. 'I don't know. I hear the words, but they're not clear. But it's something dangerous. Something important.'

'The elixir?' guessed Kassia.

'More than that,' said Jed. But how could anything from his memory be more important than the elixir?

The train slowed again and Dante gestured for them to disembark. They climbed the escalator and stepped back outside. Jed tried to relax into the feel of the fresh air on his face. Before it had made him feel alive, but even that was failing now.

Dante led them across the street and towards a huge, grassed space. It was clear that the industrial area was now some sort of public park. A canal ran alongside the open space. Dotted across the vast expanse of grass were various unusual sculptures. It wasn't clear to Jed what any of them were. And it wasn't clear to any of them where exactly Giseppi was likely to be waiting for them, if he really was.

Dante led them past a red, metal construction that looked like a flight of stairs going nowhere. Near to that was a sculpture made of scrapped wood and broken packing cases.

'Are we sure this is right?' signed Kassia. 'How will we find him?'

'Maybe it's like Prague,' suggested Dante. 'Maybe we need to find the sculpture or structure that speaks the clearest to you.'

Jed wasn't sure he was getting any messages at all from the twisted piles of metal and thrown-away wood. But that's all there was. No gasworks laboratory. So what had taken its place?

The three of them walked together just as they had in Prague. This time, Jacob wasn't with them and his absence was a painful reminder of all that had happened. They passed each sculpture and Jed could feel Kassia's hope and expectation radiating from her like heat. But there was nothing. No connection at all.

And then Jed peered into the distance and the world shifted and twisted in front of him. It was as if the earth below his feet was buckling and folding. He sank down, thrown to the ground, landing heavily on his knees. All the air left his lungs.

Jed understood in that moment why the memory from the gasworks was about more than the elixir. It was about life and death. But not just for him.

Jed tried to pull himself up but an invisible weight pressed down on the space between his shoulder blades, pinning him to the ground.

Kassia knelt beside him. 'What is it?'

'The dragon,' he spluttered.

'In your mind?'

He pointed forward. Across the park in front of them, standing apart from the other sculptures and statues, was an enormous metal dragon. Its body was green; made of corrugated iron. Blue spiked teeth jutted from its jaw; silver pipes made its eyes, and orange metal corkscrewed away from the body in a twisted tail.

Kassia linked her arm around him. Dante did the same from the other side and together they helped Jed walk towards the gigantic metal structure.

This was the place, he knew it. Where the laboratory from his memory had been so many years before. The dragon was waiting.

As they moved closer, Jed could see that metal stairs had been cut into the body of the sculpture. They led from the ground up to an open space inside the dragon's head. A man was standing at the top of the stairs. It was Giseppi. He nodded in their direction.

Jed staggered towards the stairs. He grabbed hold of the handrail, and with Kassia and Dante behind him, he began to climb. Every step hurt him. Every pull of his body was harder than the one before. But he climbed the body of the dragon like he'd climbed the O2 in London, the Petřín Tower in Prague and the Eiffel Tower in Paris. He climbed until he'd reached the very top because that is where he knew the answers would be. At the peak. The zenith.

When he reached the last step, Giseppi reached out

his hand and steadied him.

Jed took a while to get his breath. Then he looked at Giseppi, expectation and hope flooding through him.

Giseppi smiled. 'Welcome home, Fulcanelli,' he said.